Manuel Vázquez Montalbán lives in Barcelona where he was born in 1939. He is a journalist, novelist and creator of Pepe Carvalho, a fast-living, gourmet private detective. Montalbán has won both the Spanish Planeta Prize and French Grand Prix of Detective Fiction for his thrillers, which are translated into all major languages.

**Also by Manuel Vázquez Montalbán
and published by Serpent's Tail**

Murder in the Central Committee
The Angst-Ridden Executive
Off Side
Southern Seas
The Buenos Aires Quintet

AN OLYMPIC DEATH

MANUEL VÁZQUEZ MONTALBÁN

Translated by Ed Emery

Library of Congress Catalog Card Number: 2003111413

A complete catalogue record for this book can be
obtained from the British Library on request

First published in this English translation in 1992
by Serpent's Tail, 4 Blackstock Mews, London N4 2BT
website: www.serpentstail.com

First published as *El laberinto griego*
by Editorial Planeta, Barcelona, 1991

First published in this 5-star edition in 2004

Printed by Mackays of Chatham plc

10 9 8 7 6 5 4 3 2 1

For Angel Zurita,
as agreed

Mais l'angoisse nomme la femme
Qui brodera le chiffre du labyrinthe

[But anguish names the woman
Who will embroider the motif of the labyrinth]

René Char, *En trente-trois morceaux*

'My name won't mean much to you. The name's Brando.'

'Marlon?'

'That's an old joke. No, Luis. Luis Brando. The name won't mean much, as I say. True, eh?'

No, it didn't mean much, and the name's owner wasn't in the business of offering clues. Not at the start, at least. But then he began to open up.

'Have you heard of a publishing house by the name of Brando Editions?'

'Film books? You do film books?'

'No, for goodness sake...' The man was momentarily put out, but he obviously enjoyed this game of surrounding his name with a touch of mystery and uncertainty. 'It's my daughter. I have a daughter. She's giving me a lot of trouble. Would you be able to call round to see me? In your professional capacity, of course.'

'That goes without saying. I don't practise as a father. Or as a disinterested friend of fathers either.'

'Naturally not.'

It also seemed something of an effort for him to spell

out his address, as if either he didn't remember it well
or he was ashamed to be living on a run-of-the-mill
residential estate. Carvalho hung up and swung round
in his seat to face in the direction of the kitchenette.

'Biscuter. The onset of moral repression is confirmed.
Another father wanting somebody to keep an eye on his
daughter. Ever since the Soviet Empire went down,
morality has come back into fashion.'

There was no reply from Biscuter. Instead there was
the sound of someone knocking at the office door, and
even though Carvalho thundered 'Come in' the two
shadows outside didn't budge, preferring to announce
their presence opaquely through the glass.

'Come in, I said!'

Only four, or maybe five times in his life had he
experienced such a pain. There are women who give
you an actual pain in the chest when you contemplate
the contours of their flesh, and they need hardly even
look at you for the impact of the bullet to break your
breastbone and for a gentle asphyxia to deprive your
lungs of air. But sometimes all they have to do is just
stand there, just make an appearance, without giving
you the time to work out the reason why: it is their
presence, their way of being in the world that makes a
vacuum of time and space and triggers the primal angst
of the first man at the moment when he was summoned
by the first woman. Part of this, or all of this, happened
as Carvalho watched the woman take possession of his
premises, with her straight back, and her head held
slightly back in order to launch an all-embracing gaze
around his office, while she locked away her body with

her arms folded in front of her. He felt so disturbed that at first he felt fear, and then an annoyance, directed partly at himself and partly at this disruption of his equilibrium. Weeks later, when the woman remained only as a hazy outline and Carvalho was trying in vain to reconstruct her in order to store her away in some bitter-sweet corner of his memory, he had the time, and he used it, to analyse that presence, like a man trying to analyse the bomb that has just killed him as he was in the process of dismantling it, and noting in his hand the weight of each element, and its volume and texture. But now, as the woman advanced towards his desk, all he could do was lean back in his seat in an attempt to gain distance, space, and time in order to fill his chest with air and his head with words.

'Can I help you?'

And it pained him to have to invite her to sit down, because it would cut her down to half her stature. She was so beautiful that it took Carvalho a moment or two to register that she was accompanied. Her eyes were made of precious stones that had as yet been classified by no geology known to man; she had dark, honey-coloured hair, which was thick too, like the best dark honey, and which caressed her head, the head of a beautiful goddess; and she had the skin of a ripe peach and a mouth that kissed her words as she spoke. Stop looking at her, Carvalho told himself. But he carried on looking at her, and would have carried on even longer if her companion had not intervened and required his attention elsewhere. Philosophers say that good would be incomprehensible without the contrast of evil, and the same is true of beauty in relation to ugliness. Her companion was not so much ugly as counterposing a restlessness to the image of placidity which she radiated. He was one of those types who look at everything but take in nothing, with eyes that were almost devoid of eyelashes, and an unruly shock of hair, the only feature that contrived to escape the constraints of his physical and psychological discipline. He was not the sort to hand out words or gestures in excess, and this, combined with the fact that his Spanish was not as good as hers, was probably the reason why all he said was:

'Mademoiselle Claire Delmas, and Monsieur Georges Lebrun...'

They were the first French people who had ever sought to hire his services. In order to make things easy for Carvalho, they made reference to a fleeting acquaintance Carvalho had once made, in the Thai jungle more or less on the borders with Malaysia. He reconstructed the encounter in his memory, and what came to mind was an encounter with a curious post-revolutionary character, haunted by a two-fold fear — of getting old, and of becoming bourgeois. According to Monsieur Lebrun, the man was now working as an economist in the Rocard government.

'I thought he had a big thing against governments.'

'He still does. Governments are full of people who are sceptical about governments. Are you a fan of political philosophy?'

'When I hear the word philosophy, I reach for my gun.'

'No need to go that far, but it's your gun, so you can do what you like with it, I suppose.'

Then the man appeared to switch off, and allowed a long moment of silence before Claire began to speak, as she did, in the end, with a voice that was light and sensual, to match her image as a woman of the dawn.

'I'm trying to find a man.'

'That's a good start,' thought Carvalho, although, as far as he could judge, he wasn't the man she was looking for.

'In Barcelona?'

'In Barcelona. He's the man of my life.'

Carvalho understood why it was that the French were the first Europeans to discover the tango, way before the First World War, according to what he had seen in a book which, however, he had not finished reading, and which, as soon as he found it, he would use to light his next fire.

'Mademoiselle Delmas's story is very literary, I should warn you. In fact, Mademoiselle Delmas herself is very literary.'

This aside came from the reticent Frenchman, as if he suddenly felt that his presence was required in the conversation. The woman didn't appear bothered by his sarcasm. It appeared that the two of them got pleasure out of needling each other.

'Whereas Monsieur Lebrun believes only in facts. That two and two make four, for example.'

'Well maybe that's why I've managed to avoid my life being turned into a Greek tragedy. Do you enjoy reading, señor Carvalho?'

'I burn books.'

'If you burn them, it's because you have them.'

'I doubt that you'd find the story of my life particularly interesting.'

'I'm sure that Mademoiselle Delmas would. She loves other people's life stories; that way, when she runs out of her own stories, she can use theirs. I asked you whether you like reading because I like reading, and one of the most rewarding books I've ever read is *Homo Faber*, a novel by a Swiss writer, in which he tells the Greek tragedy of a man who didn't believe in Greek tragedies. Ever since then, not only do I not believe in Greek tragedies, but wherever possible I try to avoid them. That's not the case with Claire because this whole story is to do with a very handsome Greek. I'm rather curious about what you said about burning books. I also have an unusual relationship with books.'

'Sadistic.'

'Yes, sadistic, quite possibly, Claire.'

'You don't love books; you don't love anything, or anyone if it comes to that.'

He nodded in agreement, and something approaching a smile rendered the non-specificity of his features even more indistinct.

'Do you know what this lunatic does with books?'

'I can't wait to find out.'

'He sneezes on them, he takes the ripest fruit that he can find in the market and eats it over open books so that the juice dribbles over them and stains them, and he never keeps more than ten books in his house at any one time. He buys them, he sells them, or he throws them out or gives them away.'

'He gives away books full of snot and fruit stains?'

'I try to give away the least dirty ones, but sometimes I'm not too scrupulous, and when all's said and done a book is like a closed box anyway — the reader almost never knows what he's going to find between its pages. You have to take that chance.'

The woman laughed wholeheartedly and looked at her reticent companion with a certain tenderness, to which he replied with the slight smile of a young boy surprised in his secret vices. Next they're going to ask me to marry them, Carvalho thought, and part of his repressed impatience must have become visible, because the woman now made an effort to concentrate on the matter in hand.

'I think I should say at once that everything I'm going to tell you is true, because sometimes even I think that it could be untrue, a product of my obsessions. I first met Alekos, the man of my life that I mentioned, five years ago. He had just arrived in Paris, and happened to visit the museum where I was working. He was a Greek immigrant, older than myself, and was learning to paint; he was finding it very hard to survive in Paris. In fact, we had scarcely known each other for ten minutes when he was already asking me to invite him out for a meal. I thought this was a bit forward of him, but he was very handsome. He had the body of an adolescent Greek athlete, despite the fact that he was almost thirty, but at the same time his face was that of a modern-day Greek sailor, sun-tanned, with a big Turkish-style moustache, and the beginnings of a receding hairline. When he took his clothes off, he had a powerful young body — and the head of a Turkish pirate. A week after we met, he came to live in my apartment in the Marais, bringing with him everything he had. I'm not referring so much to material objects, because he didn't have many. He brought his whole cultural and emotional world. He made me feel Greek. It was as if my house, and I myself, had become a kind of Greek colony where he came and went as he fancied.'

The man applauded with his fingertips.

'Claire, that's the best version of the story I've heard yet.'

'I replaced my friends with his friends, my memories with his memories, my tastes with his tastes, to such an extent that I even changed the food I ate. For several years I went from one Greek restaurant to another, and in my kitchen at home I did nothing but Greek cooking. Do you like Greek cookery?'

'It's OK for summer holidays.'

Monsieur Lebrun again applauded with his fingertips, but this time chose not to join in the conversation.

'I adapted my life's programme to his. Not only was I fascinated by him sexually, but I also felt a kind of guilt. He used to say that the rich peoples of the world were responsible for the poverty of his own people. He appreciated you Spaniards, because he used to say that you're like the Greeks: first you made history, and then you suffered it. But the French, the Germans, the English, the North Americans and the Japanese were the present-day villains of history, and we were all responsible, and all had to pay for it. Every now and then I had a sense that he didn't love me, that in fact he was possessing me, colonizing me, and I used to tell him so. I would get hysterical and desperate, and then he would turn moody and jealous — he was jealous, very jealous, to such an extent that he didn't like me looking at other men, and every night I used to have to give him a report on everything I had done during the day. '

Her companion had got up, and while Claire was talking he went nosing about the four corners of Carvalho's office. When he reached the curtain which led into Biscuter's little world, the cubicle which housed the toilet, the kitchenette and just about enough space for the little man's bed, he reached out a finger to move the curtain aside, and found himself face to face with Biscuter, who was listening in on the conversation. He let the curtain drop back without batting an eyelid, and turned towards Carvalho to see if he had been watching him. He had.

'Don't worry, he's my assistant, and listening behind curtains is part of the terms of his contract. Come in, Biscuter.'

The little man came in, drying his clammy hands on his trouser legs, then raising them to his head to control the handful of hair that still remained on his head. He closed his great baleful eyes at the moment that he took Claire's hand by the fingertips in order to raise it to his lips and murmur:

'Mamuaselle.'

Then he did a half turn to face Lebrun, but this time limited himself to bowing his head, a touch overdramatically, Japanese-style, in order to shake the hand which the Frenchman found himself obliged, somewhat unenthusiastically, to offer.

'Messieu.'

Biscuter paraded the little French that he still had from the days when he used to steal cars in Andorra, and their French visitors were open-mouthed in the face of this avalanche of sounds, which they imagined to be somehow related to Esperanto. The intonations were extremely, in fact excessively, French, and had something of the quality of a concrete-music opera. Their visitors' tolerance was obviously being tested to the limits, so finally Carvalho intervened to put an end to the torture.

'Biscuter, our clients need something in addition to your excellent French to remind them of their homeland. I think it would be a suitable hour for a cool white wine. What French white wines do we have cold?'

'A Pouilly Fumé 1983, a 1984 Sancerre, and a 1985 Chablis.'

For the first time Carvalho noted a perplexity in the eyes of Monsieur Lebrun, who was doing a quick visual inventory of everything around him, and evidently what he saw did not square with the conversation about wine which the detective was pursuing with his subhuman assistant. The Frenchman's first snap-shot took in a down-at-heel 1940s-style office which looked as if it had come from an auction of leftovers from a Bogart film set. The second snap-shot was of the state of penury that prevailed in Carvalho's wardrobe, which Monsieur Lebrun presumed had been bought from end of season sales. As for Biscuter, the last time the little man seemed to have dressed himself was some far-distant day at the end of the 1950s, and he had apparently not removed any of his clothing from that day to this, not even to wash. On the other hand, the fastidiousness and neatness of the detective's strange assistant might have led one to suppose that when his clothes went into the washing machine, he went in with them. The third photograph took in what he had seen on the other side of the little curtain. The fourth photograph took in the four of them in the room. How was it possible to be drinking a glass of Pouilly Fumé in a place like this, and served up, what's more, by a man who looked like Fu Manchu's manservant?

'Have no fear, Monsieur Lebrun. Appearances can be deceptive. Biscuter is an excellent cellarman. Every three months I send him out on a wine-tasting trip round some part of the world. Within the limits of our possibilities, of course. I don't run to *grands crus*, but every six months or so we like to open something rather special. The last one was a 1966 Nuits-Saint-Georges. Excellent. If you are the kind of people who enjoy a white wine between meals, and something tells me that you are since both you and the lady are very literary, might I recommend a Meursault, a Sancerre, or a Pouilly. The Chablis, I think, would require the support of some seafood, or some other appetizer with a fairly strong flavour.'

'The Pouilly, if that's all right.'

'Certainly.'

'I don't understand how you Spaniards can drink any

wine other than Vega Sicilia. My grandmother was from Valladolid, and I still have the taste of Vega Sicilia in my mouth from my childhood.'

So, a girl from Valladolid.

'And what do you make of Greek wine?'

'Greek wine was the one thing that might have put Claire off her Greek tragedy, especially the one they make with resin.'

'Some of the wines from Crete are fine, and the sweet wine from Paros is good for desserts. But Alekos used to make me drink Demestica, the most common wine in Greece, because he used to say it was a wine of the people and a wine for stupid tourists, and that when he returned to Greece he felt that he was a mixture of a man of the people and a stupid tourist.'

'Was he a communist?'

'His father had been a communist guerrilla, and later spent a few years in prison. Alekos had been a member of the Party's youth section, but he went off politics when they made it legal. He came to France. He was more an anarchist than a communist, really.'

'The most innocent of ideologies and the most useless.'

'You'll never understand him, Georges. You're a salesman. A buyer and seller. A trader.'

Biscuter arrived with the glasses and the bottle of wine, and also brought a dish of savoury biscuits spread with a pink paste, which elicited a joyous cry from the woman.

'Tarama! How wonderful! How did you manage to produce a tarama in such a short time?'

'These are the small advantages which come from

having my assistant listening behind the curtains. It's a rather unorthodox tarama because it's not made with grey mullet roes. Like most people, Biscuter uses cod roe.'

'Tarama takes me right back to Greece.'

And her eyes became the colour of the Aegean, while you could see the gentle rise and fall of her chest beneath a woollen jumper which covered two substantial breasts which Carvalho guessed were well-rounded, with untipped nipples, like a teenage girl.

'Tarama, moussaka, dolmades ... all we need now is a bit of Theodorakis, maybe the *Periyiali*, with the words by Seferis ... Alekos used to put it on the record player every now and then and play it until "his ears began to cry", as he used to say.'

'How did you manage to lose such a fascinating man?'

'A man doesn't find other men fascinating, unless he's a homosexual. But even though you meant it jokingly, I can promise you he was fascinating. In fact I didn't lose him. He left me.'

'Why?'

'It was my fault. I put too much pressure on him, and maybe I confronted him with a reality that was too much for him. The first years were years of a mutual possessiveness, all very conventional, very much "a couple for life". Then he took me to Greece to meet his parents, and with that trip I ended up becoming a daughter-in-law. My in-laws still write to me, and my mother-in-law cries every time she remembers how Alekos went off and left me. We'd been living together for three years when I first noticed that the quality of our relationship was beginning to deteriorate. He was spending more and more time outside the house, although it was also the case that he was becoming economically more independent. He was earning a bit of money posing as a model. As I told you, he had a very beautiful body. I saw how the sexual side of our relationship was falling off, and how he seemed to be losing his capacity for fantasy. He was like an actor who is just going through the motions. I inherited something from my Valladolid grandmother — a bad temper, I suppose — and I'm not a prudent woman when it comes to matters personal. So before long I started demanding to know why his feelings towards me had changed. I fell into the old cliché of asking him who the other woman was — I took it for granted that there was another woman, you see. And instead of reassuring me, or forcing me to face the truth, he let me shout and scream, left me going out of my mind, and kept me in a state of uncertainty for a whole year, until I began to suspect that maybe it wasn't exactly what I had been thinking. Alekos was very much one of the boys with his friends, and, as you may know, Mediterranean men are very natural and affectionate with each other. They hold hands down the street. They kiss when they meet. They give each other tender looks, and the western point of view finds all this a bit off-key. One day I'd told Alekos that he and his friends went round like a gang of gays, and he seemed to find this very amusing. He said that capitalism had only allowed us to maintain eroticism in our reproductive organs, and even that was only allowed for as long as they needed manpower. As soon as they had too much manpower, they even started trying to control our reproductive organs. Anyway, I started following him, day after day, to such an extent that I began to neglect my work at the museum, and it was fast coming to the point where they were going to sack me. In the end I came to the conclusion that it wasn't a matter of another woman. He was continuing to see his friends, and there were always new faces around — usually young Greeks who needed assistance from the group, because not all of them had proper French residence permits. Everything seemed to be just the same as before, and this depressed me even more, because I thought it was all my fault; I began to blame myself for the breakdown of the relationship. I started carrying my displays of tenderness to excess, and my sexual demands too, to such an extent that he felt cornered — maybe overwhelmed is the word — and started becoming defensive. This made things even worse. One afternoon when I was supposed to be at work I was feeling very depressed, and I decided to stay at home. I had the lights out because my eyes were so sore from crying. Alekos arrived, and didn't notice that I was up in the bedroom. He sat down at the dining-room table and began to write, and from the bed I could see his handsome profile, and the handsome sadness of that afternoon as he wrote, and I watched as the sadness turned into anguish. He began to cry, with great heavy tears which rolled down his cheeks and soaked the paper. He was crying from what must have been a deep personal anguish, the way that you only cry when you're in love. He wasn't crying for someone who'd died. It was for unrequited love.'

'Claire, allow me to interrupt, and to observe to you, and to señor Carvalho and his illustrious cellarman, that you have described a scene that is totally post-Romantic in its inspiration. If it wasn't for the southern seas, and heavy warm tears, and casks of ship's biscuits and salt meat, and pale señoritas walking under parasols, a fair part of the literature of the nineteenth century wouldn't exist. You have just demonstrated the extent to which the literary education which we receive in our high schools and universities is based on the nineteenth century. A weeping Greek! That's an orientalist portrait painted by Delacroix and penned by Lord Byron. If you had spent time on your literature course studying Artaud, Genet or Céline, you would never have come out with a description like that. Literature and films give us a framework of images with which to construct our lives and our memories. Why don't you put all that nineteenth-century nonsense behind you and try and describe the same scene as seen by Robbe-Grillet, for example. If you'd read more Robbe-Grillet, you wouldn't be running around after such an excessive Greek.'

'Do you mind if I continue, señor Carvalho? I wouldn't want you to get the wrong impression of us. Georges enjoys the role of trying to drive me to distraction, even though he knows that he can't.'

'You see, Carvalho? You see the foursome that we're playing out? What actors could do our parts best, would you say? She is Ingrid Bergman, without a doubt. Your assistant could be Peter Lorre, albeit a trifle thinner. You yourself are Humphrey Bogart to a T, a role that you have evidently studied for. And as for myself? What actor could play my role? I realize that I'm putting you in a tricky spot, because this is going to force you to commit yourself to a physical and moral judgement about me.'

'I have a terrible memory for films. As far as I'm concerned, John Wayne and Anita Ekberg are one and the same, and Elizabeth Taylor is actually Lassie . . . wasn't it Elizabeth Taylor who went across the whole of England on four legs in *Lassie Comes Home?*'

'I'll tell you who could play your role: Peter O'Toole dressed up as Bette Davis.'

Something approaching mortification sealed the narrow lips of Georges Lebrun.

'We left the man of your life, the Greek, crying his heart out as he was in the process of writing a love letter. Who was he writing to?'

'That was precisely the problem. I fell asleep, and he didn't wake me up when he realized that I was in the house. I waited for him to go out, as he did on most nights. But he didn't. He came and lay down next to me, and very soon fell fast asleep. After a while I got up, quietly, and went to find the letter. It was tucked between the pages of a poetry book, a book of Alexandrian poets contemporary with Cavafy, and including Cavafy himself. The letter was written in Greek, and the only Greek I knew was tourist Greek — hotels, customs, that sort of thing. But I was beside myself, obsessed, and I went to what I thought was the safest place in the house and set about deciphering the letter with the aid of a dictionary. All the verbs came up in the infinitive, but I was getting results. As the early hours wore on, I began to unravel the meaning of the letter. It turned out to be a love letter, a love letter addressed to a man, who as far as I could see was called Dimitrios. Later on I found out who Dimitrios was — he was a young man who had recently arrived from Samos, whom everyone was trying to help, because he was in pretty bad shape. He was a drug addict, and a painter like Alekos. But that night all I knew was that I had a proof, although I suppose it was only a half-proof, really, because my mastery of Greek left me only at the gates of truth. The letter was filled with eroticism, but a dream-like eroticism, more or less platonic. It was a description of one of Alekos's dreams. Dimitrios was the object of his desire, and he was reproaching him for being so off-hand with him. It was the letter of a jealous man. The jealousy which he had once devoted to me, he was now devoting to this young man. But when I read the translation to myself, as I must have done a thousand times, I still had hopes that it would all turn out to be a passing rapture, that the affair had not been consummated. I couldn't bear to think of Alekos in bed with another person, let alone with another man. The letter gave no indication of the extent of their physical contact, and I concluded that it hadn't yet happened. But at that point I made a mistake, because from that night onwards I did the worst thing I could have done. At every available opportunity I began to criticize homosexuality in front of Alekos, and he reacted angrily and dismissively. Why not homosexuality? It was the only sexuality which society could not approve of. It's not productive. Not reproductive. It's the only radically revolutionary sexuality, that's what Alekos said, and his tone was too impartial, too neutral for him not to be involved in what he was saying. After a few weeks of hurling accusations and abuse at each other, I finally confronted him, although I never admitted that I had read his letter... probably because I'd read it in the toilet — "retrete", as you Spaniards call it — what a revolting word. It's got such a terrible sound to it.'

'Almost nobody in Spain calls a "retrete" a "retrete" any more. In fact nobody in Spain calls anything by its real name these days. Almost everyone says "lavabo", which is a word as pasteurized as "toilet". People nowadays want to forget that they shit, that they piss, that they fuck, and that they die.'

'From that day on I lived a life of suspicion and torment, and the fact that Alekos was non-committal drove me even crazier. As time passed I realized that he was deliberately pushing me to the limit so that I would be the one to break off our relationship.'

'Was that the way it happened?'

'No. I felt neither humiliated nor insulted. I was simply in love and didn't want to lose him. But life was obviously becoming impossible for him, and one day he left me. He went to live in the studio of a friend of his, but this friend wasn't the person that his letter had been addressed to. I wanted to kill this Dimitrios. I put a knife

in my handbag and set out to find him. I hurled abuse at
him like a drunken whore, and then, because my hands
were trembling, the knife fell to the ground, and I
started to cry. I played out every kind of scene imagin-
able, including one night when I ended up sleeping in
the doorway of the house where Alekos was living, in
the hope that he would take pity on me. I even tried to
kill myself . . .'

'And it was at that point that I came on the scene.
Allow me to re-introduce myself, señor Carvalho,
because perhaps you've forgotten the name. Georges
Lebrun, chief sales representative for the French Television Corporation, on a special commission in this
future Olympic city, to negotiate exclusive rights for a
number of educational sports programmes which we
are hoping to develop after the Olympics. Every
Olympics casts a shadow, and it is in that shadow that
one makes or loses money. Mademoiselle Delmas was
my next-door neighbour, and on the morning of 14th
March 1989 the concierge of the building came and
knocked me up, to help save this young lady's life,
although in fact we then discovered that she hadn't
swallowed enough pills to kill herself. She had simply
wanted to bring herself to the attention of her Greek,
instead of which all she managed to do was wake up the
concierge and her next-door neighbour. Actually,
waking me up is easy enough; I don't sleep a lot at the
best of times. As you can see for yourself, Mademoiselle
Delmas came out of the experience in one piece, and
from that moment on I took her under my wing, not
exactly out of sexual interest, nor even for humanitarian

reasons; if you knew me well, you would know that I have no pressing sexual urges, and that I am devoid of humanitarian impulses. On the other hand, I have a great curiosity for the animal behaviour of human beings, particularly in the field of emotions. Reason is programmed and enriched by culture. But emotion is not. What distinguishes man from animals is a sophistication of emotion, and how emotion gets turned into culture. How much longer was my neighbour going to continue pointlessly moping around? How many tears would she shed before she contracted ocular hypertension? How many times would she come and weep on my shoulder, even though she knew perfectly well that when I get near tears it makes me sneeze? It's a reflex action that I've had ever since I was a child. I have to confess that Mademoiselle Delmas is very persistent in her desires and her misfortunes. She felt very wretched about her Greek disappearing, and she suffered all through what was left of 1989. Come the New Year, she seemed more resigned to it, but this last spring she received news that he had moved to Spain, to Barcelona in fact, and this promptly produced in her an obsession with chasing after him, finding him, and asking him to start again. Let's not forget that he was the man of her life, and you only live once.'

'And you have to learn to love, and to live.'

'Was that a line from a song or a poem?'

'A bolero. A song.'

'Yes . . . songs can be extraordinarily profound sometimes. Mademoiselle Delmas was looking for a suitable opportunity to come here, and in the end I was able to offer one. I had been commissioned by French television to negotiate with the Olympics Organizing Committee a contract for a set of programmes. This involved getting together a group of experts, and among those experts I nominated Mademoiselle Delmas in her capacity as museum director. Obviously they were a bit surprised at my choice, because neither the kind of museum that she ran, nor the place that she occupied in the hierarchy, really justified her being part of our commission. However, then I tried the old trick of hinting to my superiors that Mademoiselle Delmas and myself were lovers. All I had to do was smile discreetly as I mentioned her name. An Italian would have given a knowing wink.'

'A Spaniard too.'

'We French are more refined, you see. All it takes is a slight smile when one mentions a woman's name. Then you cropped up in the course of a conversation with this man who knew you. It appears that you had an interesting encounter south of Bangkok, and you travelled on to Malaysia together.'

'In those days he was a Taoist.'

'First he was a Maoist, then he was a Taoist, and these days he's in the "I'm Alright Jack" party. He was one of the last utopians to give up the ghost: he kept the faith from May 1968 right through to June 1985. Until the twelfth of June, to be precise. He was having a cele- bratory night out in a high-class fish restaurant in Les Halles in Paris, and he let it be known that he was transferring his allegiances to possibilism. And of course, possibilism starts with oneself. He came to see me, and I gave him a present of the dirtiest book that I had to hand. A novel by Marguerite Duras, which in those days one was expected to have read. My friend, or should I say our friend, had become so proper and conventional that he was incapable of turning down my disgusting gift. When he left he simply tucked it under a table napkin. Marguerite Duras never knew about this, and I trust she never will. I hope you'll promise me that.'

'I promise.'

'And you too, Claire.'

'I promise.'

By now there was not even a trace of tragedy in the woman. She actually seemed to be rather enjoying herself, and she observed the two men as if they were about to be her companions in some great adventure.

'Where do we start?'

'Good question, Carvalho. We don't have a lot of time. I can't extend my trip beyond a fortnight, and even that is stretching it; I will be making other trips, but unfortunately I won't be able to pack Mademoiselle Delmas in my luggage. The Greek is wholly her business. He's not the kind of person for me. My flavour is more lily of the valley and the songs of Mistinguette.'

'Where do I begin?'

This time Carvalho addressed himself to Claire, and he watched as she reached into her handbag and pulled out a photograph, with both hands, as if she were raising the Holy Grail.

'This is my man.'

Carvalho had seen hundreds of characters like this

trying to chat up tourists in the Plaka in Athens. They probably came from some bio-genetic cloning plant run by the Greek government, specializing in breeding studs, although Carvalho could see that the mature face in the photo looked interesting. The Greek was good-looking, prematurely aged, and each of his wrinkles probably indicated some failure in his life, in the same way that the rings of trees tell you how old they are and the deformations in their bark indicate where they have been mutilated. From the moment he set eyes on the photograph, Carvalho saw the man as his victorious rival, the kind of rival who won't even deign to recognize you as a threat.

'Anything else? Do you have any other information to be going on? What kind of circles does he frequent? Have you been to the Greek consulate? Have you been in touch with the embassy in Madrid?'

'All that's been done, and nothing came of it. Nobody knows how he got into Spain, there's no record of him at the border, and he has avoided the Greek and French authorities. We just know through my in-laws that he's in Barcelona, because every now and then he writes to them from here, but he never gives a return address. His only skills are posing and painting. Would you say that's sufficient to go on?'

'No. But I'll have to make do with what we've got. Where can I find you?'

'We're staying in the Palace Hotel. You'll find Mademoiselle Delmas in Room 313, and myself in 315. The wine was excellent.'

So said Lebrun, having drunk the last drop from his

glass. Thereupon he got up, evidently expecting Claire
to follow suit. But she was still setting about the last of
the tarama tapas. She ate prettily. She moved her lips as
if she were whispering to herself, and her cheeks as if
she were caressing herself from the inside. Carvalho
was suddenly assailed by a sense of the ridiculous, and
as he took his eyes off the woman he caught the look
that was coming his way from the Frenchman. 'You're
hooked, friend,' said Lebrun's lashless eyes, and there
was no way Carvalho could deny it. There was one
savoury left on the tray, and she asked:

'Can I take it with me?'

'Biscuter, wrap it in some tinfoil for the lady.'

'If she wants, I could make some more, boss. For the
journey.'

'The lady isn't going on an expedition. She wants it as
a family memento.'

Claire put the little package in her handbag and
bathed Carvalho in a wash of sweetness and gratitude
that stayed with him for several hours afterwards,
although when he looked back later the main thing that
he recalled was the words that she had said as she
turned at the door.

'Find him, please. Dead or alive.'

It's rather harder to find someone dead than alive,
Carvalho thought as he switched off the light to give
himself the solitude that he required. The pair of them
could have been plucked from the pages of a serialized
romantic novel, and there had been nothing to clarify
the nature of the relationship that bound them. They
were friends; they were resident in Paris; they were

neighbours in Paris, in fact; and they were accomplices in the search for Alekos the Greek. He was going to have to embark on a terrain that was unfamiliar to him — Olympic painters, Olympic wheeler-dealers, dealers in Olympic culture — in order to find an ambiguous Greek, of whom it wasn't clear whether he was homosexual, or whether he had just got tired of women who were too beautiful and too possessive, and instead had fallen platonically in love with a disdainful Greek adolescent. Who could he turn to for help in a situation like this? He ran through a list of painter friends, and the only suitable name he came up with was Artimbaud. He also considered those comrades of yesteryear who were now working on the preparations for the Olympics, and this provided him with an extensive list of possible contacts. In this city, you were either working for the Olympics, or you were dreading them — there was no middle ground. The '92 Olympic Office, the pre-Olympic Office, the post-Olympic Office and the trans-Olympic Office, were now employing people who in normal circumstances would be the least Olympic of anybody. They had gone from Marxism-Leninism to democratic progressivism, and now to an involvement in the preparation of all the various Olympic events which Spanish democracy would host in 1992. The Fifth Centenary of the discovery of America, the International Exposition in Seville, the Olympics, and Madrid as Cultural Capital of Europe. Anyone who has not spent at least half an hour of their lives preparing for revolution will never know how you feel when, years later, you find yourself employed in preparing showcases for prize athletes from the worlds of sport, business and industry. From the Sierra Maestra to Mount Olympus, from the Long March to the marathon. From the clandestine crossing of frontiers to negotiations with representatives of the world's drinking-chocolate manufacturers who are all chasing the Olympic concession for cocoa. Once again, out of the complete collection of betrayers of the Sierra Maestra and of Long Marches, he settled on 'Colonel Parra', who, in former times, had been the author of a manual on torture, written on the basis of his own experiences, and who had now been recycled into the job of handing out sponsorships. Nowadays Artimbaud was definitively on line and even had an answering machine. Carvalho left him a message which he deemed sufficient for the purpose:

'I'm trying to get in touch with a Greek painter by name of Alekos Farandouri, probably without a residence permit, and possibly gay, although you wouldn't think it to look at him. Alive or dead. Ring me.'

On the other hand, getting through to Colonel Parra involved a kind of bureaucratic hurdle race to get past five thousand secretaries who all sounded the same and who all used the same delaying tactics.

'Tell him that Gorbachev's ringing to offer him the concession on alcohol-free vodka.'

'What company did you say you were calling from?'

'The Warsaw Pact.'

'Is that a musical group?'

'Not exactly.'

Colonel Parra was missing somewhere on the western

slopes of Olympus. However he would be happy to see him at ten o'clock the following morning, ten on the dot. Carvalho contacted Biscuter to sound him out on developments so far. Recently Biscuter had been going through a personal crisis, because he'd decided that Carvalho set too little store by his opinions. Charo was going through a crisis too, and Bromide was dead. Maybe it was Carvalho who was provoking all this crisis, by feeling himself increasingly bored with his own rituals, and increasingly disenchanted with other people's. God is dead, Man is dead, Ava Gardner is dead, Marx is dead, Bromide is dead, and I'm not feeling too good myself, he thought. Biscuter congratulated him on the fact that his reputation was now crossing international borders, and then retreated into a state of mute abstraction.

'Is that all you have to say?'

'Without wanting to upset you, boss ... I realize that you meant well, but I didn't like the way you showed me up because I listen behind the curtains.'

'But he was the one who found you out.'

'He acted like he hadn't seen me, but you had to go and show me up.'

'You were the queen of the party, Biscuter. Your choice of wines bowled them over, and you saw what a hit you had with your tarama. What did you make of the woman?'

'Don't get me wrong, but I was more interested in the man. I've seen him in a film somewhere, although I can't remember which one. He looks like a German spy.'

'So the Germans are spying on the Maginot Line again. What do you imagine they might be spying on in our part of the world?'

It really did appear as if she had made no impression on Biscuter. Carvalho couldn't make up his mind what instructions to leave in the event of Charo ringing, probably because he was hoping that she wouldn't, so he went to get his car to drive home to Vallvidrera. His head was full of fragments of their conversation, and in his mind's eye he carried the image of Claire's face, her geological eyes, that mouth that ate so prettily, her static sweetness, and the deep passivity of a kind of a woman open to total passion.

'Dead or alive.'

As he went through his front door he already knew what he was going to do. Pick out a few pale aubergines and make himself a moussaka; then get *Zorba the Greek* and *The Four Horsemen of the Apocalypse* from his bookshelves and burn them. Layers of aubergine, lightly fried, layers of seasoned mincemeat, layers of fried onion, tomato, a touch of garlic and sage, and then the whole covered with bechamel and grated cheese. A de luxe moussaka, which would bear little relation to the doleful slabs that you usually get served in tavernas in Greece. He had no Greek wine to hand, but he did have a Sicilian Corvo de Salaparuta, which was an adequate substitute. As the moussaka began to absorb the heat of the oven, he went to sort out the books and flicked through their pages to find reasons to justify his decision to burn them. There was the tango announcing the outbreak of the First World War in Blasco Ibañez's

Four Horsemen of the Apocalypse: 'A new pleasure had arrived from beyond the oceans to make men happy. People would ask each other, in the mysterious tone of initiates in a moment of mutual recognition: "Can you tango . . .?" The tango had taken over the world. It was the heroic hymn of a humanity which somehow focused its aspirations in that harmonic strutting of the hips . . .' And then there was the philosophizing of Zorba the Greek, the elegy offered by this strong, tender male to Madame Bouboulina, the old French lady to whose homage Zorba constructs the metaphor of life in a leaf of a tree: a worm devotes its entire energies to getting through the surface of the leaf in order to find out what mysteries lie at the back of it; finally, having sur-mounted all the difficulties, it gets to the other side, straightens up, looks around, and discovers that this side looks exactly the same as the side it has just left, which means that he has to face up to his own failure. He wondered whether, allowing for a difference in age and beauty, Claire wasn't perhaps a kind of Madame Bouboulina, a western woman with a guilt complex, fascinated by the legend and the prospect of des-truction by the barbarians. He put the books on the fire. The wood was just beginning to crackle when the phone rang, and at the other end was an Artimbaud who was more in the mood for conversation than for dealing in concrete information.

'Just a minute, don't think me rude, but what do you know about this Greek of mine?'

'I suppose you think you're going to find a Greek on every street corner. I'll ask some of the younger painters. These days painters of my generation all drink mineral water and they're all waiting for a slice of the action on the Olympic murals.'

'You too, Francesc?'

'Me too, Carvalho.'

And just as he was beginning to nod off, with his mouth full of the taste of sage and two glasses of ouzo, which he had left over after a trip to Mount Athos with Artimbaud, the final call of the night arrived:

'Are you asleep, boss?'

'Not now, I'm not.'

'It's just that I've remembered the person in the film I was trying to think of. That Frenchman is a dead ringer for the boss of the gambling house in *Gilda*. Do you remember it?'

'Are you referring to Rita Hayworth?'

'No. Rita's the woman.'

'Are you sure, Biscuter?'

'Sure.'

'If you say so.'

Too much villa for too few servants. The woman who opened the front door was dressed neither as a maid, nor as a gardener, nor as a female factotum; on the other hand, judging by the way she led him across the garden and made him wipe his shoes on the mat, one could have been forgiven for thinking that she had personally given birth to the entire Brando family. Surly, single-minded, checking to right and left to make sure that nobody had altered the existential equilibrium in the small portion of the universe which she oversaw, and so uninterested in her intruder that she was more or less happy to let him pass through her morning, through the garden and through the lives of the Brando family without even bothering to remember his name.

'What did you say your name was?'

'Carvalho, Pepe Carvalho.'

She walked on tiptoe across the floor which had obviously cost her a lot of effort to polish, and she left Carvalho costing the quality of señor Brando's fixtures and fittings. A mixture of tradition and design council awards; furniture that had been passed down from his grandfather, or somebody else's grandfather; and modern furniture that provided living proof that Barcelona is one of the five thousand capitals of international design. However the place was short on harmony and long on collector's mania and suggested that its owner was concerned to display a good taste which would stand the test of time. The lady disappeared through a door, and then reappeared on the threshold in the manner of a nurse in a high-class private clinic.

'Would you be so kind as to step this way?'

She let him pass and closed the door behind him with such care that Carvalho found himself more concerned with the quality of the wood, for fear that it was going to crack, than with the man who was waiting for him at the end of an office that was too large for a private residence, an office typical of a thousand and one pseudo-intellectuals who worry because their true talents have never been recognized. In a lifetime of observing other people's offices and other people's toilets, Carvalho knew that pseudo-intellectuals are as solicitous about the one as about the other, and that sometimes they contrive strange syntheses which for some reason have never made it to the pages of *House and Garden.*

'I'm a failure. My wife left me for the first time a fortnight after our wedding . . . Anyway, never mind that. Before we start, would you mind going down the corridor and opening the second door on the left. Don't forget, the second door on the left, and I'd ask you to open it suddenly. And if it's not too much to ask, would

you mind walking on tiptoe until you get to the door ...
Don't forget, you have to open it suddenly.'

He may have been a failure, but the office desk was
made of some highly expensive wood, and so was the
bookcase, and the lampstand was of some semi-
precious metal. In other words, he had the look of a
client who was solvent and willing to pay for Carvalho
to play the idiot tiptoeing down a corridor and suddenly
flinging a door open. Carvalho did precisely as ordered,
until he arrived at the door; here he paused and applied
his ear to the wood, which smelt of expensive polish.
Either it was a very hifi recording, or there was
someone screwing on the other side of the door, with
the rhythmic perfection of Swedish gymnastics and the
panting of people who have graduated in the arts of
secret pleasures. There was no question of turning
back. He overcame the false modesty of the gilded
doorknob, and pushed with his shoulder. The girl was
impaled on the sex of the elderly man whom she had
beneath her. She was blonde, she had pear-shaped
breasts, and she must have had rapid reflexes, because
she instantly turned to the door and left off panting in
order to shout:

'Daddy, you're a bastard!'

As for her ageing partner, he wrinkled his brow, and
who could say whether this was in an effort to identify
the face of the intruder, or because he had achieved
orgasm? It occurred to Carvalho to apologize, but then
he simply closed the door gently and returned to the
office where the self-styled Brando was awaiting him,
confident in the outcome of his little initiative.

'What did you find there?'

'A young girl . . .'

'Sixteen years old . . . My daughter.'

'. . . making love . . .'

'Fucking.'

'. . . with a gentleman who looked rather annoyed.'

'A man old enough to be her father.'

Brando was now satisfied. He was neither tall nor short, neither fat nor thin, an extrovert, and the kind of man who is inclined to tell it like it is, in the manner of Navarrans and the Aragonese. He informed Carvalho that he was from Navarre, but that his name was Central European in origin.

'Brando. So now you know the name, eh? Quite amusing, your crack about Marlon.'

This moment of self-satisfaction then gave way to renewed melancholy.

'I'm a failure. My wife left me for the first time a fortnight after we were married; then she came back to me, and we had a son, who has just taken over my business, and then this daughter into the bargain. My daughter was just ten years old when my wife left me for good and went off with a gymnast who had come twenty-sixth in the world gymnastics championships. His speciality was the rings. But he ended up taking a bad fall that left him paralysed, and my wife took over his gym. I never really understood that. For all the time we lived together, the nearest she ever came to doing sports was trimming her nails and putting on make-up. Do you like women with make-up?'

Carvalho shrugged his shoulders.

'You're more or less the same age as me. Wouldn't you agree that the best thing for a woman's face is soap and water?'

At the risk of repeating himself, Carvalho shrugged again. Then Brando muttered something to himself. His lips moved but whatever it was he said was not audible. There are some days when patience definitely becomes a virtue in a detective's line of work, so Carvalho allowed himself to be seduced by the splendid softness of an armchair that was more quilted than upholstered, and settled in to wait for Brando to return from his voyage of the mind.

'Most mornings the girl comes to my office for breakfast in the company of her latest conquest. She picks precisely the moment when she knows I'm going to be there, introduces us to each other and obliges us to start a conversation, all the while treating the pair of us as if we're her favourite people in the world. I've always behaved like a modern father to her, very understanding and all that, and I had to put up with the two or three boyfriends she had at the end of the summer term two years ago. At the start of the first team of the following year, she turned up here with one of those characters who do radio chat shows and reckon they can sort the world out in one hour flat. He was a short chap, with a grey beard and a Catalan accent. I showed her the door. Several months later she turned up again, this time pregnant, not by the chat-show man, but by somebody else whose name we never found out. I sent her off to London with a female cousin of mine. I'm sure I don't need to tell you why.

And since then I've turned a blind eye, and I'm even willing to put up with conversation at breakfast time. But things have taken a bit of a turn.'

'Are you referring to the elderly gentleman who was in bed with her?'

'No. That's the least of it. He's a splendid man, and he knows how to listen. He treats her like a father. I hope the thing lasts ... although sometimes I think that she's using him against me. Every chance she gets, she starts making these horrid comparisons. "Alfredo's the same age as you, Daddy," and things like that ... Things that are calculated to hurt. He wouldn't. He's a gentleman.'

'So what's the problem?'

The moment of truth had arrived. Brando assumed an air of great sadness.

'The other night she was picked up during a police round-up. The police were looking out for illegal immigrants, foreigners without papers, and she turned up among them. I went to get her out, but she wouldn't explain what she was doing there. The police told me that they'd occasionally seen her hanging about in the area, and they had her down as a high-class girl looking to score drugs ... You see? But one thing I know for sure — she's not on heroin, and she's not on cocaine. It's obvious that she's not on heroin, because sometimes when she's asleep in bed I go in to cover her up, and I take a look at her arms. And the fact that she's not doing cocaine is as sure as my name's Brando. I like my coke, and I can tell someone who takes the stuff from someone who doesn't. I've been taking it for thirty years now and I can guarantee you that she's not on cocaine. But I'm worried by the way she's hanging round these barrios. What's she looking for? I tried to find out from Alfredo, the gentleman who's in bed with her, but he spun me a sorry tale, a very sorry tale. The girl hardly talks to him. She fucks him, brings him to me for breakfast, and then forgets all about him until the next time she happens to phone. So where would you begin?'

Carvalho began by setting out his financial terms. Brando did his sums with the aid of a wristwatch calculator, and having added, multiplied and totalled, he gave Carvalho a long hard look. It was obvious that he thought the detective wasn't up to the price, but then he nodded in agreement.

'OK, I think we can do business together.'

Hunting for a Greek — two Greeks in fact — and protecting an oversexed young lady from herself, was maybe a bit much to be taking on all at one go, but his French clients were ships in the night, and Carvalho knew that he depended on a local clientele for his living. Nonetheless, he decided to put the case of the wayward daughter on hold, and apply his undivided attention to the cosmopolitan undertaking which had been the source of Biscuter's irritation. His first job was to see Colonel Parra, who was now head of one of the hundred or so offices servicing the hundred or so organizations dedicated to guaranteeing the smooth working of the Olympics. 'Colonel' Parra had been wearing a tie for the best part of twenty years now. He deserved credit for having been the first revolutionary to don this particular item of apparel, when he had

landed himself a job in the research department of one
of Spain's biggest banks. However these days he liked
to wear what was definitely an archetypal tie, one of
those ties which are intended to signify culture and
class, one of those ties whose quality is recognized only
by experts in ties. What's more he had a habit of
touching his tie as if it was a sexual organ, or as if he was
a member of the masonic lodge of natural silk ties. He
had aged, but his ageing had been relativized by the
modernity of his tie. He was obviously keen to get shot
of Carvalho, and at the root of this desire was probably
the racial superiority of a thoroughbred owner of a
Gucci tie in the face of a Carvalho who had put on the
only tie he possessed, a skinny low-grade Thai silk tie,
more a holiday souvenir than a proper tie.

'Georges Lebrun? Allow me to hunt in a haystack for
a month or two to see if I can find this particular needle.
Do you have any idea what you're asking? Do you know
how many foreigners we have in the city at this
moment, all trying to get a piece of the Olympic action?
An Olympics needs everything from a thimble to an
elephant. Well, I have a complete collection of thimble
salesmen, and another collection of elephant salesmen
too.'

'This one sells culture.'

'In that case let's look in the culture file. France. ORTF.
Do you have any idea how many proposals we've had
from French television?'

'You know my limitations.'

'Georges Lebrun. Producer of educational films on

the Olympics. Just a moment, and I'll get my secretary to run him through the computer.'

'First feed into the computer whichever one of your five thousand secretaries has to put it in the computer.'

'Pepe, you're behind the times. You should bear in mind what Herbert Spencer said: either you grow, or you die.'

'In my day, Spencer was seen as a proto-fascist.'

'These days he's seen as part of Spain's heritage of social democratic pluralism. And that's the way it's going to be for a good while yet. Don't fight it. Lie back and enjoy it. Either you progress, or you die. Don't forget, the Berlin Wall is no more.'

'I see you're in good shape, Colonel.'

'Spare me the sarcasm. I left that particular army years ago.'

He dictated various instructions down an intercom which itself appeared to be wearing a tie. Everything in that office seemed to wear a tie.

'The challenge of the Olympics is quite terrifying. Nineteen ninety-two will be a decisive year for us. The eyes of the whole world will be on Spain.'

'The first time that's happened since the Civil War. I believe that was the last time they thought us worthy of the front page of the *New York Times*.'

'Nostalgia is a mistake, Pepe.'

'And what about irony?'

'Empty sound.'

From a printer located behind Colonel Parra, an invisible man, or perhaps an invisible woman, began to issue forth a tongue of paper, which suddenly came to a halt, in a moment of telluric silence. Ex-Colonel Parra reached out one arm, without turning his head, and tore off the sheet with the precision of an expert. He read what was printed on it, but then withheld the information from Carvalho while he took a long look at him.

'What do you want this for? I can't let information go out of this office just like that. You do realize that we close deals worth hundreds of millions of pesetas here, every day?'

'It's to do with one of my clients. It's got absolutely nothing to do with your multinational Olympic enterprise. It's all to do with a Greek, a poor Greek, who's on the run from a woman. He's not even an Olympic Greek.'

'You promise?'

Carvalho gave him a look that said 'I promise', and was rewarded with Lebrun's file: 'Georges Lebrun, age 39, born Paris. Assistant director-general at the ORTF. Name of firm: Olympia 2000. Educational videos on the Olympic spirit, to be based on filming the Olympics in Barcelona. Pre-sales already arranged with forty countries. Confidential economic report AYF36. Positive evaluation C. Cont. file 62.'

'It doesn't say anything here about how he dribbles snot and fruit juice over books. Your computer is shit. What else does it have to say?'

'Nothing else.'

'Do you have any personal impressions of Monsieur Lebrun to offer?'

'Why would I? Personal impressions are of no use to me. I meet upwards of fifty people a day in this job.

Who's going to retain personal impressions? He's a functionary, and I would say he's very able. He speaks a language of facts, which we process in our computers. I'll probably have lunch with him one of these days, if the computer throws up a promising connection and if my political bosses give the go-ahead.'

'Who are your political bosses?'

'Nani Gros, Tere Surroca and Pasqual Verdaguer at the head of it all. You might remember them as Chou En-Lai, Zhdanova and Melancolico, which were their *noms de guerre.*'

'What particular *guerre* was that? I'm inviting you to dinner one of these days. At my house if you like.'

'I only eat Italian salads and grilled blue fish.'

'Why blue?'

'They tell me they're good for cholesterol. I don't have cholesterol yet, but prevention's always the best cure. So, everything OK?'

'Fine. I'll ring you.'

'My secretary will have to make the appointment. I do a lot of travelling. I'm off to Seoul in a couple of days, to check out the effect of the Olympics there.'

'In the same way people will be coming here to check out the effects of the Olympics on us.'

'Tomorrow's another day.'

Carvalho left the office trying to inject an athletic spring in his walk so as to keep face with the young men gathered there, even though they appeared to be as short on muscle as they were long on ties. He had arranged a rendezvous with Artimbaud in the Pa y Trago restaurant, and was looking forward to a lunch that would be substantial and imbued with solidarity, with somebody who wasn't scared of dying before the expiry of his three-score years and ten. But he found the painter looking so thin and contained in his clothes that he understood at once that he too had gone over to the side of gastronomic repression, to the side of the living dead, of the tyranny of food fundamentalism. The painter ordered a pitiful portion of fromage frais and a coffee with no sugar, and tried to avoid looking at the calf's head casserole which Carvalho ordered. The detective gave a brief account of the matter in hand, without going into details about his clients, but he did mention his meeting with Pedro Parra.

'I don't know him. I'm in the plastic arts section.'

'Sounds horrible.'

'But it's true what you say. Everything that moves in Barcelona these days is at the service of the Olympics. You have people coming to buy the place, people coming to see it all, and all the rest of us trying to sell it. There's not one artist in this city who's not looking out for what he can get out of the Olympics. The lion's share is going to go to the architects, but they'll also be needing sculptures and murals.'

'I don't think that my Greek is likely to figure among the chosen few. He's come here running away from something, or looking for something.'

'If he's modelling, he'll probably be doing it at one of the Fine Arts schools, either the official ones, or the less official ones, or maybe at EINA which is just down the road from your place. But from what you tell me it's more likely that you'll find him doing portraits for tourists around the cathedral, or the Sagrada Familia. Until a month or six weeks ago you would have found it easier to find him. At the moment people aren't out walking so much, what with the roadworks all over the place. Trying to find him by his nationality is going to be like playing Russian roulette. You'd have to go poking round in all the corners where artists are trying to survive, and ask if they've got a Greek there. People say that we've never earned so much money by painting, but at the same time we've never had so many painters with nothing to say. It took me twenty years to achieve a certain financial security. These days, if an artist hasn't hit the big-time by the age of twenty-five, he sees himself as a failure.'

'And what does he do once he sees himself as a failure?'

'Probably carries on seeing himself as a failure. Pepe, I don't understand these young painters, and I'm beginning to worry. All my life I have struggled for every kind of painting to be accepted, even during the times when there was a total dictatorship of abstract painting — the days when if you happened to fall foul of two or three critics, you'd starve. But these days any pea-brain can dip his cock into a paintpot and do a *Homage to AIDS*, and the next day his picture's hanging in some museum.'

'When people start comparing nowadays with the old days, it's a sure sign that they're getting old. I know it's unavoidable, but it's best to keep quiet about it and never make a virtue of it. I've always been an unusual kind of detective, but if I were to tell you how the big investigative agencies have got the business all sewn up, you'd hand me a thousand pesetas and suggest that I take up carol-singing instead.'

'We artisans are a dying breed. We should stick together. Is the meat good?'

'Why don't you order a portion for yourself?'

He closed his eyes, only re-opening them to order a salt cod with chickpeas and a bottle of red wine.

'I won't be eating dinner today.'

When a person fills his stomach with the fruits of the sea and the earth, and thereby alters his mood, he confirms the opinion of those who say that there is no effect without a cause.

'You should go and see Dotras, a painter friend of mine. He's my generation, but he's pretty way out. Likes to think he's still young. If your Greek exists, Dotras is bound to know him, and if he's a homosexual, even more so. Not that Dotras is a homosexual, but his wife loves them, and she enjoys seducing homosexuals by playing the maternal role. Once a woman's past the age of fifty, what else is there to do?'

'And Dotras just looks on?'

'Dotras is resting. If you knew him, you'd understand.'

The artist whom Artimbaud had mentioned lived in an obscure alley at the back of Plaza de Medinaceli, midway between the Barcelona that was rediscovering the sea at the Moll de la Fusta, and the Barcelona of the heavy drugs, the muggings and the bag-snatchings around calle Escudiller and Plaza Real. Big old decrepit houses built for rich and poor alike in the seventeenth and eighteenth centuries. No speculator's bulldozer had thus far dared to touch them, which meant that there were still courtyards full of weeds, peering out from their enclosing walls like nature's protest against the teeming city. Shops full of cheap biscuits and sausage that was sold a few slices at a time to old folk and immigrants who were fleeing from geography or from the police records of the bargain-basement section of Interpol. Perhaps because it was an unsellable piece of inner-city real estate, in those big rambling houses you could still find fine spaces for artists — both practising and would-be. Dotras had been one of the most promising painters of the 1960s, and was now doing very nicely, thanks to an extremely supportive clientele which comprised, among others, a large number of rich gays, whom his wife fussed over and cultivated as if they were prize roses. As a result he had dedicated part of his output to painting portraits of the mothers of gays, and athletes who had been overcome by efforts that remain unspecified. His speciality was an automatist technique which involved covering a board with oil paints, and then placing it on top of huge sheets of cartridge paper which he laid on the floor. Then he would roller-skate to and fro over it with a rhythm reminiscent of a flamenco dancer caught between improvisation and epilepsy. He had never sought to sell these paintings, but kept them stored in a warehouse which he kept locked, with a bunch of enormous keys, so that they might one day be inherited by the eight children he had had with three different wives, five of whom made up the rock band Muscle

Power, while the other three held senior positions in the
Catalan Savings Bank. One had even made it to
managing director. Carvalho knew nothing about him
except what Artimbaud had told him, but no sooner
had he crossed the threshold of Dotras's studio than the
painter handed him a curriculum vitae that had been
written for him by one of the five thousand best poets in
Andalucia, in exchange for a painting.

'It's always as well to know who you're talking with.'
This was said by a man who was dressed in a waistcoat
of heavy cretonne which looked as if it had been stolen
from a museum of anthropology, and he himself
looked as if he had escaped from the same museum on
a day when the anthropologists' backs had been turned.
He had a powerful shock of tousled grey hair over a
face that was dark-skinned by birth and had been
further darkened by the sun which he emerged to take
every day down by the port, 'because the sun is the god
of life, and if I had been an Egyptian, I would have been
one of the devotees of the sun cult. I'm a great one for
mythology.' The woman had free-falling hair that
reached to her waist behind, and two enormous
breasts, equally free-falling, which reached to her waist
in front. She was wearing a black robe held in by a gold
cord, and multi-coloured sandals. She barely greeted
the new arrival, preferring to continue her conversation on the phone which was the only thing in that
enormous studio not intimately connected with art.
Canvases, and paintings, some completed and some
half-finished, easels and palettes and splashes of paint
all over the place, like the remains of a feast of colours,

and a short staircase which led to the loft where Dotras had sired his last five children with this latter-day Valkyrie.

'This place is the heart of freedom in this city. It was much more so fifteen years ago, when we were all naïve and believed in the resurrection of the just. There aren't many islands like this left in Barcelona. This is Dotras's island, where you can come to lose yourself, if you want, but where you can also find things. What are you looking for?'

'A Greek.'

'Remei, do we have a Greek?'

'Two,' Remei replied, without removing the phone from her ear.

'You hear that? If Remei says so, then it must be so. We've even had Iranian princes here, and various lovers of the Empress, a very available lady by all accounts.'

'Farah Dibah?'

'No. The Shah's mother. She even used to screw dwarfs . . . You're not from Barcelona, are you? From Zamorra, perhaps?'

'No. Why?'

'These days it seems like everyone comes from Zamorra. Do you know where Zamorra is?'

'No. But I know they do an excellent wine.'

'Nobody knows the place. It's like a Spanish version of the Bermuda triangle. Are you a travelling salesman?'

'No. Artimbaud sent me. I'm looking for a Greek.'

'Oh yes, I remember. We've got two. What sort of Greek are you after?'

'He's got the body of Antinous and the head of a Turkish pirate.'

'So he's a half-breed. Remei, which of our two Greeks has the body of Antinous and the head of a Turkish pirate?'

'All Greeks are the same,' replied Remei, still on the phone. It was at this point that Carvalho got up, went over to the woman, took the phone out of her hands, hung it up, and confronted the Valkyrie by more or less pressing his nose against hers.

'I need to speak with you.'

'Have we been introduced?'

'They tell me that every spring you go out shopping with the local gays.'

'I was always cut out to be a mother. If Dotras hadn't ended up impotent, I'd have had twelve children by him by now.'

'It's the chemicals in the paints. They make your pecker go limp,' said Dotras, putting one hand to his sex.

'My gay friends don't grow old, unlike some people I know.'

'Not everybody sees it the same way. I'm looking for a Greek with the body of Antinous and the head of a Turkish pirate.'

'Anything more than that to go on?'

'He's called Alekos. He's a painter, and sometimes does modelling. He might be homosexual.'

'Alekos,' Remei murmured, as if she was filing the name in her memory.

'I used to be very keen on a Greek singer called Alekos Pandas. He used to sing at the Festival of the

Mediterranean. At the start of the sixties, when I was young. Where were you in the summer of 1962?'

'In prison.'

'A criminal?'

'A communist. Then, and as the years went by I began to settle down.'

'We could use someone like you at our party,' Dotras shouted, from his perch way up on a scaffolding where he was working on one end of an enormous canvas. 'Come along tonight. Sometimes we get Greeks coming along, and sometimes Mohicans. They're always the latest in Greeks, and the latest in Mohicans. We drink plenty of Alella wine, and we smoke innocent marijuana, like the barrack-room marijuana of the 1940s. That's all. We don't take heroin in this house, and we have no racial prejudices against Greeks or Turks. Tonight my children's group will be performing — Los Musclaires — and my other children, the conventional ones, will bring their wives and children and cakes and muscatel, because we're coming up to All Saints and the Day of the Dead. Do you have AIDS?'

'I don't think so.'

'We don't allow anyone with AIDS in this house.'

'Nobody,' Remei reiterated, returning to the telephone and reoccupying her own time and space.

'Should I bring anything for the party?'

'Yourself, some friends, two thousand pesetas a head, and a bottle of something special to surprise us with.'

'What would you say to a twenty-year-old bottle of Knockando whisky?'

'Friend, if that's what you're planning to bring, we'll treat you like a tsar!'

Carvalho emerged from the labyrinth of alleyways, and having tried four telephone boxes before finding one that worked, he managed to leave a message at the Palace Hotel. He arranged a meeting with Claire and Georges for ten o'clock in the Casa Leopoldo, to be followed by a lavish party at the studio of an artist who collected Greeks.

'Make sure you get that down, he's a collector of Greeks,' he stressed for the benefit of the receptionist who took the message. Then he drew up a programme for killing what was left of the day in such a way as not to disturb the eagerly-awaited emotion of his next encounter with Mademoiselle Delmas. He passed by the office to see if anyone or anything had been caught in Biscuter's telephonic spider web.

'Mr Brando has rung several times, asking to speak to you.'

'Why do you call him "Mr"?'

'With a name like that, what am I supposed to call him?'

Mr Brando. He couldn't decide whether to respond to the vengeful father's calls, or to ignore him, because either way there was little to report on the basis of what he had done, or not done, so far. He was annoyed at the thought that it might interfere with his relationship with Claire, and with the Greek, but on the other hand he had time on his hands, and he decided to visit the first logical contact in his researches into the nocturnal activities and infidelities of the young, wayward sexual dynamo. Like mother like daughter, perhaps; maybe it was the mother who was the bearer of the chromosomes of amorality which the daughter had inherited, given that the father didn't seem to have contributed much to the girl's psyche. The gymnasium was surrounded by white Opels and Volvos. There was nobody in reception, and Carvalho was able to penetrate as far as an enormous window which took up half a wall and which gave onto a big hall where about twenty women in coloured leotards were attempting to follow the instructions of a lady instructor. Despite the fact that there were some very good-looking bodies there, along with others of a depressing mediocrity given the cars they owned, it was inevitable that the Peeping Tom's gaze should settle on the lady instructor and on the strong, shapely body of a woman of about fifty, with a mane of dyed platinum blonde hair which protruded above her harpie's face like a kind of crest. From her lips fell fierce injunctions, insults and familiar diminutives.

'You, Merche, move your arse... What on earth's the matter with you, Pochola? Is that an arm or a stump you've got there...? Come on, let's see your head up... Let's have you breathing properly — the air is free, for God's sake...'

Not a hint of rebellion among her victims.

'Lula, this is supposed to be a gymnastics class, not a slow-motion session...'

Their muscles were going through such pain that her acid comments came as a welcome diversion. The instructor limited herself to demonstrating how the exercise should be done and then patrolling up and down among her flock with a baton which she used to prod the various parts of their anatomies which were out of condition or not able to do the exercise as she had wanted it done. It was as she was pacing up and down that she saw Carvalho behind the window. She shouted:

'Tradesmen deliver on Wednesdays, and I pay on the twentieth of the month!'

She turned on her heels, confident in the effect of her words. However, when she turned to come back down the line she saw that Carvalho was still standing there. Angrily, she threw her baton down and came storming across to sort him out. Her suffering clientele took this opportunity to break ranks, to abandon their gymnastic poses, and to collapse on the floor to enjoy its hard, welcome coolness. She was just about on top of Carvalho when it occurred to him that attack would be the best form of defence. The woman was taken aback by her apparent inability to instil terror in her visitor, and was even more disconcerted when Carvalho bent reverently over her ring-bedecked fingers and made as if to kiss her hand. In the event the gesture came to nothing, partly because it was never Carvalho's intention in the first place, and partly because she withdrew the threatened appendage as if someone had just dropped boiling oil on it.

'Didn't you hear what I said?'

'Señora Brando?'

'Señora who?'

It was not so much the words as her tone that

prompted Carvalho to suggest that they find a more private place to talk. She was about to dismiss his suggestion until she saw that her clients had suddenly recovered from their tiredness and were crowding up against the glass to get a better view of the action. A single glare was sufficient to send them all back to their positions, and then a grunt signalled to Carvalho that he was invited to follow her. The office that she took him to was graced by the curious presence of a man in a wheelchair playing patience at a coffee table. The woman stroked his head in passing, to which the man barely responded, and she sat herself down behind a desk piled high with papers. Her sagging facial features were a clear demonstration of the failure of vast quantities of make-up to make good the ravages of long years of married life.

'What does that bastard Brando want now?'

'Do you see your daughter often?'

'She's the one who comes to see me. When she needs money. And in particular she comes to see this sorry specimen, because he gives her whatever she wants.'

The 'sorry specimen' turned his head. He still had the smile of the day when he had come in twenty-sixth or twenty-seventh in the men's world gymnastic championships.

'You may laugh, but the little good-for-nothing knows how to get money out of you!'

There was a tenderness in the voice of this fearsome creature, and Carvalho allowed her to sound off for a while about the shortcomings of the Brandos of this world, and how unfair it was that she now had to take responsibility for her daughter. If the police arrested her, it would teach her a lesson. Nobody ever learns lessons like that at second hand. She knew nothing about her daughter's secret life. The girl's brother probably knew more.

'Ask his majesty for an audience, and he may see fit to grant it ... Every once in a while he tries to pull the girl into line, but he always does it by putting the rest of us down — his father and me. If you ask me, he's no son of mine. I'm a person who likes to tell it like it is.'

From what Carvalho could see, there was something of a family pattern here, a pattern which was capable of surviving the test of divorce. Or maybe when you have two human beings who are addicted to telling it like it is there's no way out for them other than divorce ... or planning an imperfect crime. No, she didn't believe that the girl was looking for kicks. She wasn't that kind of girl. She had so much life in her already. The invalid seemed to go along with this and nodded in agreement.

'Look how he drools every time I mention the girl.'

'But she must be looking for something.'

'That's for sure. The girl tends to get what she wants. Never puts a foot wrong. She might seem a bit flip as she goes through life, but not a bit of it. When she wants something she goes for it, and she's got it by walking over the corpse of her father. Wouldn't you say that he looks like a corpse these days?'

If he'd said yes, they would have been friends for life. The three of them. Because the invalid card-player, one time twenty-sixth or twenty-seventh in the men's world gymnastics championships was dancing in his wheelchair, evidently delighted with what was going on around him, as if he was enjoying Carvalho's company and the civilized tone that his wife had suddenly adopted. She was as happy as he was, and went over to him, smoothed down his ruffled clothing and stroked his head again.

'He hardly says a word. But he says what he needs to. Disabled men make the best husbands, you know.'

'Ring your daughter. Talk to her woman to woman. Ask her what she thought she was doing hanging out with drug dealers and riff-raff.'

'She'll turn up when she needs money. And I won't be the one who gives it. He will, though; he'll give her whatever she wants, without a murmur.'

'Will you ring me?'

She nodded yes, and that concluded their audience. She went ahead of Carvalho down the corridor, and stopped just before a window that opened onto the sweaty madhouse, which her clients had now gathered around gossiping. They were exchanging the small understandings they had gleaned from their lives as rich, bored housewives.

'Look at them, like parrots.'

'You treat them very harshly.'

'At the start I used to treat them very considerately, and they started taking liberties. They're spoiled rich kids who've never grown up. But if you shout at them a bit it keeps them in line. They come here when they've had enough of their masseurs and jacuzzis. They need someone to treat them like army conscripts. That's what they need — a two-year spell in the army would do them all a power of good.'

He left the lady instructor plotting further cruelties against this collection of the city's most select bodies. All this gymnastics had awakened his appetite, and he couldn't decide whether to drop in at La Odissea to enjoy Antonio Ferrer's *cuisine d'auteur*, or to give it a try at the Nostromo, which was run by two sailors, one by the name of German, and the other Basora, who never failed to add Lorca to any conversation he had with Carvalho.

'But the night becomes interminable when they rest on the sick, and there are ships that seek to be looked at in order that they can sink in peace.'

In Carvalho's head their conversation had been accompanied by a day-dream about Claire. She appeared as a sensual, playful doll, first in an old photograph, then moving about, then in the foreground, and then with an empty country landscape as a backdrop. By then, Carvalho had consumed half a bottle of rum, and when he went to freshen his face in the wash-room, surrounded on all sides by engravings of sailing ships and shipwrecks, he saw the face that was reflected back at him from the mirror and he decided that Lorca's lines were probably meant for him . . . 'There are ships that seek to be looked at in order that they can sink in peace.' He surrendered himself to a double game of allowing himself to be swept along by his emotions and at the same time being ironical about them, in order to prevent himself feeling ridiculous, and to re-establish control of his situation. He wished Basora luck, and promised to return one day to empty his bottle. 'My bottle,' as he repeated several times, as if he was drunk, as indeed he was. He wandered around a series of alleyways that had been abandoned to their own pointless history, and decided to go and take a look at the city that was being rejuvenated to function as an Olympic showcase. In the middle distance the cathedral now overlooked the excavations for an underground parking lot which would allow the city to increase the number of its Japanese visitors. 'We apologize for the inconvenience.' 'We are working for you.'

'Barcelona, look your best.' 'Barcelona, more than ever.' The whole world seemed to be in transit, in passing, including the city itself, which was in a phase of transition between a known past and a future that had no defined limits. Claire was passing through too, and as he moved through this city, in part deconstructed and in part reconstructed, he felt like an adolescent boy waiting for the encounter with the girl who is going to make him adult and unhappy, that girl who suddenly disappears, and whom he might catch up with thirty years later, when it's too late for just about everything. He heard himself start singing an old bolero, emboldened by the alcohol that was reaching into his brain. 'What a pity ... Why didn't you tell me? If I had known, I would have been all yours.' Señor Carvalho, if you had given me even the slightest hint of your feelings, I would have abandoned my once-in-a-lifetime Greek and I would have offered myself to you, as the prize at the end of the labyrinth, your reward for all your efforts in your search for the truth. Do you know what *alezeia* means in ancient Greek? If he was capable of asking the question, even though he had placed it on Claire's lips, it's because he knew, or had at some point known, what *alezeia* meant in ancient Greek. Maybe he would finally meet Claire at the end of the labyrinth, once her business with the Greek had been sorted out. If he did meet Claire one day in the next thirty years, he felt sure that it would not be in a station somewhere, but in some cemetery. Maybe I'll finally see her again when she comes to place flowers on somebody's grave and passes close to mine, and something tugs at her memory and makes her stop for a moment: Carvalho? Pepe Carvalho? That name rings a bell . . . Or maybe Carvalho would manage to live for another thirty years, to run into Claire on a pavement somewhere. By then she would be well on the way to old age herself, and she would help him across the street, and he would make an exception, and would behave like a gentleman and allow himself to be helped, instead of giving her a whack with his stick. Carvalho knew that his capacity for day-dreaming, for imagining and predicting the finale of this strange emotional caprice, would lead inevitably to the burlesque and a sense of impotence that strangely pleased him. Nothing like this had happened to him for years, and he felt more ridiculous than guilty. He only felt guilty about having been excessively honest with himself in not phoning Charo because he hadn't wanted to subject her to the hypocrisy of a solicitude which he didn't feel. He felt cruel, legitimately cruel, in the way that only a rational animal can feel when it has fallen in love. The more the feeling grew, the less ridiculous it became to admit it to himself. He suddenly met himself as a different man, something more like what he actually was, when the glass of the shop windows reflected back to him the image of a man who would definitely be far too old in the year 2000, and who had never felt the slightest curiosity about what it would mean to go round that particular corner of time. As a teenager, when far from the object of his desire, he was in the habit of going down the Ramblas in the belief that somehow he was going to find her waiting for him at the harbour's edge. Carvalho had never tested this presumption to the limit, but in later years he had remained faithful to the impulse every time he found himself submerged in the bitter-sweet imbecility of love. This time, as he found himself going down the Ramblas following the trail of his adolescent self, he was able to divert his steps in the direction of Can Boadas, in search of a first martini, and if he didn't like the martinis that were on offer, he'd order the house special. A martini is like a piece of ceramics, or like country cooking; it never achieves total perfection, and you're always left with a thirst for the ideal martini. The first one they served him was sufficiently good for him to order a second, and this led on to a third. The alcohol in martinis affects your psychology more than your blood, and put him in a sufficiently sympathetic mood to strike up a conversation with a short character who was drinking a long drink with a lot of ice in his glass and a lot of sadness in his eyes.

'Alcoholics anonymous?'

'Not at all. A deputy in the Catalan parliament,' the lone drinker replied.

'A good drink between sessions?'

'No. I'm lost.'

A member of parliament, lost on the Ramblas, sitting melancholic and meditative in front of a long drink, could only be a socialist.

'Are you a socialist?'

'Does it show?'

'Socialists tend to be miserable these days. Can I buy you another drink?'

'I ought to have the courage of my convictions and chuck the whole damn thing. Capitalism has won, but it's rotten to the core. Tomorrow I have to speak in support of a bill that I don't believe in.'

'Don't get bitter with life, friend. Speak in favour of some other bill.'

'I've got no time for the others either.'

'In other words, you've got problems.'

'The communist party are all traitors. They don't want to make the revolution any more. They want to become socialists, and the only thing left for us socialists now is to become liberals. History will absolve us. It's strange, every once in a while I forget my own name, and I find myself wandering round the city. The psychiatrists say I'm suffering from a split personality. But it's not true. I'm just looking for my real personality.'

'If I find it before you do, I'll tell it that you're here waiting for it.'

'Only until two, though. This place closes at two.'

He paid his bill and that of the disoriented socialist, and followed his destiny down the Ramblas, as if arriving early would bring closer the moment of his encounter with his two French friends. At Casa Leopoldo, German allowed him to choose a table at which he would be able to down his white wine and watch Claire's entry into the restaurant. 'Very chilled, very chilled,' Carvalho insisted, 'because my head's very hot.' The restaurateur was accustomed to his excesses, which were as unusual as they were total, and left him to drink the white wine like a man drinking water. By the time his French visitors crossed the threshold that led into the dining room, Carvalho was sailing on golden seas of the best wine in the house. From the bridge of his drunken ship he was able to examine what his guests were wearing, and what he saw pleased him. She was wearing exactly the right thing for a French lady travelling aboard a drunken ship. She had on a long white jacket and a pale green silk blouse which caressed her neck with swirling ornamentations that looked like cresting waves. He had on a cream suit, with a brown shirt, a darker brown tie, and his flat, white, studiously wrinkled hat, a sum total of inconclusiveness which mirrored the inconclusiveness of his features and his gestures. The reticent prince allowed the gastronomic initiative to be taken by Carvalho and the restaurateur, and only his eyes betrayed a certain surprise when he saw the

Rabelaisian display of crayfish with garlic, squid and tiny octopuses, baby eels, duck pâté and slices of kiwi fruit, small lobsters and langoustines, and an enormous grilled flounder. While his admiration was ocular, Claire's was verbal, and when they had explored the entire range of the piscatorial possibilities of the Mediterranean, she decided that the time had come for a slight touch on the rudder, so she pulled from her bag a bottle of Vega Sicilia, and placed it on the table.

'This is a small homage to my grandmother.'

'I doubt that señor Carvalho would be prepared to allow a red wine after so much seafood and so much white wine.'

'I would permit Vega Sicilia even with fish soup. It is not a wine. It is a mark of identity: artificial, but well-executed. In the days of your grandmother, this wine did not exist.'

'It reminds me of Valladolid, and the countryside of Castille.'

'That's taking it a bit far . . .'

Carvalho had already been consuming her so much in the course of the day, without actually seeing her, that he tried to keep his eyes off her during the meal. But in every meal there comes that moment when people have to look at each other and conversation or argument has to begin. A meal can never be allowed to end in indifferent silence, unless one of the diners happens to have dropped dead. The detective provided a resumé of his results thus far, which the Frenchman listened to with a not unexpected lack of interest, and which she followed with an air of fascination rather than urgency. Perhaps she was the sort of person who would get more pleasure out of looking for her Greek than from actually finding him. Carvalho warned them that they would probably feel like tourists in Dotras's studio, but every tourist needs to break out of the confines of his hotel once in a while.

'Not always,' Lebrun chimed in, suddenly animated by this proposition. 'You never choose your cities, it's the cities that choose you. I've stayed in hotels all over the world, and very seldom have I felt strongly enough summoned by a city to feel like breaking out of the confines of a hotel. But we'll see if Barcelona is worth the effort.'

He immersed them in the belly of the Barrio Chino, in the dying embers of its cheap prostitution that had been pushed to the margins by the dread of AIDS; then, once again, the inevitable Ramblas, from which they emerged onto the harbour and the Moll de la Fusta. Neo-classical buildings in the service of military authority, the occasional touch of neo-Gothic, maritime agencies, a neo-Romantic square, a showcase for the spirit of post-modernity embodied in the way the avenue had been remodelled to culminate in the gigantic prawn by the designer Mariscal. At a point roughly equidistant from the pretentious edifice of the Post Office and the statue of Christopher Columbus, Lebrun saw fit to exclaim:

'What a mess!'

Against a background of ships, the sea, disused sheds and towers that had once served some useful purpose, they crossed the avenue, and then Plaza de Medinaceli, in search of the alley where Dotras's studio was located.

People's doors were open, and the full moon was hanging over the decrepit sheds. The woman touched all this with the tips of her jewel-like eyes and with the tips of her silken fingers, all the while smiling a gentle smile. No sooner had they penetrated the inner depths of the studio than they understood that the picture would have been incomplete without them. Here everyone was dressed as native bohemians, and they were thankful for the visual contrast provided by these tourists, evidently recently disembarked from some cruise liner and with just a few hours on shore. Carvalho didn't register in their appreciation. They must have assumed that he was a guide for one of the tourist agencies, and they preferred to devote their energies to a close examination of the luxury lady and her transient gentleman.

'It'll be two thousand pesetas a head,' señora Dotras advised them.

'What do we get for our money?'

'In no other part of the city can you see what you are going to see here.'

The Frenchman paid, and Carvalho deposited his bottle of Knockando in the hands of the painter, who was dressed for the occasion as a concert player of some obscure Indian musical instrument. The principal occupants of the place were young people, arranged in small groups and talking in low voices.

'Here we have preserved an ambience of the late nineteen-sixties and early nineteen-seventies. When all things were still possible,' Dotras informed them, raising his voice above a musical background of the

Bee Gees, the Beatles and Pink Floyd, in a space surrounded by gigantic paintings by Dotras and twenty-year-old protest posters: women pissing in gents' urinals, and 'Wanted' posters of Richard Nixon. Even the youngest of the clientele looked to have recently emerged from a long night of seventies-style revelry, and Dotras confirmed that this was exactly what the place was about.

'You won't find other islands like this in the city. Each generation has a right to its nostalgia, and ours' — the plural was intended to include Carvalho — 'is the last generation which will preserve the cult of nostalgia. Nostalgia is something one has to cultivate.'

'This man is before his time. He has created a living museum of behaviour.'

This was the first time that the Frenchman had shown any capacity for enthusiasm. They were offered rice salad and curried chicken, on the basis that such dishes were quintessentially part of the epoch that was the object of their worship, and they were introduced to a North American research student who was doing research into 'life in post-Franco Spain', for the University of North Carolina. Dotras's grandchildren were going over their grandfather's paintings with spray paint, and the Valkyrie's five offspring were tuning their instruments. The concert was to be a homage to the 'gathering of Canet', the Spanish Woodstock, actually Catalan, as Dotras emphasized to the North American, who took notes in her notebook, and to Monsieur Lebrun, who took notes in his head. Carvalho was inclined to do what he usually did when he found a

place terminally boring — leave his face there and take
his head off somewhere else. As his eyes went looking
for some nook in which to hide his head, his gaze
stumbled across a girl whom he had first seen in more
propitious circumstances. It was Beba, the daughter of
Brando and the lady instructor, lying sprawled on a pile
of cushions and chatting with a different elderly man
from the one she had been massaging the morning
Carvalho had first met her. Not so elderly, really —
more like Carvalho's age.

'Who's the girl?' he asked Dotras. The painter was
irritated at being distracted from his role as a data bank
for the University of North Carolina, and barely glanced
at the duo comprising Beba and her companion.

'I don't recognize her. Has she paid, Mama?'

His wife weighed the girl in a pair of mental scales
that were visible only to herself, and nodded that she
had.

'And who's the man with her?'

'Likewise,' insisted señora Dotras, stubbornly. The
painter redirected his attentions to the North American
social scientist, and Carvalho didn't press the point. He
decided to examine Beba at his leisure as she held forth
while her partner just sat and listened, as though he
were tired or stoned. Beba had a look of gentleness
about her, as if she were the teacher or mother of the
man who was listening to her.

'Who is that girl?'

Claire had taken him by the arm as he was watching
Beba from a distance.

'She's very pretty. Do you know her?'

'No. Or maybe yes. She's not on my agenda today, though.'

'She's terribly attractive. Very young. I find her very moving to look at. Don't you find her very angelic?'

'Probably. There are many classes of angel.'

Claire sank into a moment's silent reflection on angels.

'And what about my Greek?' Claire suddenly asked, as if suddenly recovering a sense of purpose. Carvalho discussed the matter with señora Dotras, who pointed them in the direction of a young man with big eyes, wearing a blue tunic. Claire examined the Greek with eyes which were at first evaluative, and then dismissive.

'He's not my Greek.'

'But one Greek might lead to another.'

Carvalho and Claire settled themselves on a pile of cushions next to the young man in blue, while Lebrun moved from one group to another, listening and observing in the manner of a special envoy from the United Nations, before or after some more or less corrupt set of elections.

'Alexopoulos is the most promising Greek painter I know,' Dotras announced, as he offered to introduce them.

'You never told us how many young Greek painters you knew.'

Claire laughed, and Carvalho felt suitably honoured. They sat down on the cushions, and Carvalho was about to commence with introductions. But he felt the girl's hand on his arm, and when he looked up he saw that she was asking him to let her do it. She deprived him of her beautiful eyes in order to bestow them on the Greek, who was watching them from a cautious distance, obviously aware that they were about to ask him something. She embarked on a long whispered explanation which Carvalho was not able to hear, and gradually the man's resistance melted, until finally he leaned back on one elbow and brought his face very close to Claire's, which made their conversation even more inaudible. Claire suddenly drew apart from the youth, and, squatting on her haunches, leaned forward, with a ringlet of honey-coloured hair caressing one cheek and her head immobilized by a process of reflection which Carvalho presumed must have been unshareable. She turned to the detective again, and it was as if the full moon had entered the studio from the outside and was trying to hypnotize him.

'I was right. Alekos is in Barcelona.'

'Where?'

'He only comes out at night.'

'Why?'

Something — either tears, or some internal emotion made her eyes shine even more than usual.

'He's living in an area called Pueblo Nuevo, and at midnight he goes to a restaurant in a square nearby. He said he doesn't know the name. It's at the end of the main street of Pueblo Nuevo. He lives in one of the abandoned factories there. Do you know the area?'

'I know it. Although it's called Pueblo Nuevo, there's not much new about it these days. It's an industrial, working-class area which was built up at the turn of the century. Like all things poor, it has aged rapidly, and now it's more or less just wasteland behind the Olympic Village, full of ancient factories and abandoned warehouses.'

'Where do we begin?'

'Now?'

'Now. Tomorrow could be too late.'

Carvalho would never normally have permitted a client to set the pace like this, but this woman was not a normal client.

'Let's go and find that restaurant. He says it's in a square with very big trees. They only serve cold things there — cheese, pâté, sausage, and so on. In spring and summer you can eat out. They might be able to suggest where we find him.'

As he tried to uncross his legs, Carvalho found that he was more or less crippled. His legs felt as if they were crawling with flies all eager to suck his blood. He hated cushions and low chairs; he hated Dotras and his wife, and their nostalgic charades, and he was beginning to hate the musicians, who at that moment were singing a Catalan version of *We shall overcome*, in homage, as they explained, to the spirit of Joan Baez and Bob Dylan, and also to their mother, who had brought them into the world on the same day as the famous Burgos trials against the militants of the ETA. The mother in question was now serving a mixture of orange juice and vodka, a concoction that had been in vogue twenty years ago and which, as she explained, rejoiced in the name of 'screwdriver'. The North American lady noted this with the kind of good faith unique to repentant imperialists. By this time Beba and her elderly gentleman had disappeared.

'Are you leaving already? What do you think of my concept?'

'You should get a new show, Dotras. May '68 is pretty played out by now.'

'But seeing that we've set it up, it seems a pity to change it. And anyway, it wouldn't be so easy. This summer we were looking into the possibility of doing a new "show", as my wife and I like to call it, but after May '68, what was there? Just fear. Fear of the crisis. Fear of having no money. Of not knowing the truth. Of the truth not even existing. Fear of getting old . . . But all that isn't the past, it's the present. Have you ever thought of the possibility that the past has ceased to exist? That as from now only the present exists? Have you ever thought about what the world actually is now, ever since the Berlin Wall came down?'

'I never stop thinking about it. But not at this time of night.'

'Have your French friends been enjoying themselves?'

Just as a slight smile seemed to be indicating a leave-taking that would be entirely conventional and inconsequential, Lebrun pulled a visiting card from his top pocket and handed it to Dotras.

'This is a brilliant idea you have here. Any time you feel like staging it on a larger scale, get in touch with me. A generational psychodrama, done live, with audience participation . . . Amazing . . .'

Dotras evidently had his doubts about Lebrun's

sincerity, but he held on to the visiting card as he saw them out of the door.

'Have you found your Greek?'

Claire nodded and followed Lebrun out. Carvalho found himself left behind, and took the opportunity to ask Dotras:

'Who was the Greek you introduced us to? Can he be trusted?'

'As much as any other person round here nowadays — yes and no.'

'Where are we going?' Lebrun asked, when they finally re-emerged onto Plaza Medinaceli.

'To Icaria.'

'At last!'

'That wasn't meant as a joke. There's a part of Barcelona which today is just about to disappear under the Olympic bulldozers, and which was built in homage to Icaria. It was an industrial, working-class area, naturally, which just goes to show that the Catalan workers of the nineteenth century also had dreams that one day they would reach Icaria. In fact, the Olympic village is going to be called Nueva Icaria — "New Icaria".'

'Olympia in Icaria. Like attracts like. One legend attracts another.'

'You may be interested to know that this more industrialized part of Pueblo Neuvo — Poble Nou in Catalan — used to be known as the Catalan Manchester. Barcelona industrialists in the nineteenth century hero-worshipped the English model. I like contemporary ruins, Monsieur Lebrun, and recently I have

82   MANUEL VAZQUEZ MONTALBAN

done a lot of walking round this city so threatened by
modernity. In the old barrio, very close to here, they're
in the process of driving through a road, which is
supposed to remove the bad odours of this rotting city,
although God knows where they think they're going to
remove them to. There's not going to be a lot left of
Icaria, the Catalan Manchester. It's strange how the
bosses dreamed of Manchester and their workers
dreamed of Icaria. What image would you say those
names conjured up nowadays?'

'Probably nothing at all.'

Claire walked in front of them with her arms crossed
in front of her as if she had received some mysterious
eucharist and her whole body was the tabernacle
enclosing it. They took a taxi in front of the Army
Headquarters building, and Carvalho gave the driver
their approximate destination — a square that was full
of big trees, at the end of the main street of Pueblo
Nuevo. The taxi driver gave them a critical look. They
didn't look like nocturnal muggers, and there are
always people who don't have the first idea where
they're going. There was total silence when they got
into the cab, a silence which Carvalho covered with the
same hand with which he covered his face, while
Lebrun tried to cover it with an ironic smile, and only
Claire seemed to have her sights set on something
ahead of them, as if she could already see in her mind's
eye the story that was about to unfold, a secret story
that only she knew.

'Where are we going now?' Lebrun asked, finally.

'To a restaurant where they serve pâtés and cheese.'

'More food?'

'Alekos might be there.'

This reply seemed to satisfy Lebrun, and he settled back into his seat. His eyes had turned into two slits which were filtering the landscape imagery of nocturnal Barcelona, the leafy shadows of the citadel park, the pomp and circumstance of the Palace of Justice, and when they passed the Arco del Triunfo, he let out a mild chuckle.

'So you have one too, eh?'

'Our Arc de Triomphe is rather smaller than yours, but then so were our triumphs. For the best part of three hundred years, the only triumphs we Spaniards have enjoyed have been over ourselves.'

After a while, despite the darkness of the night, their eyes began to be assailed by the ambiguity of a landscape in which it was hard to tell where the destruction ended and where the construction began. Cranes, great piles of earth, bulldozers, levelled building plots, foundations for new flats, like the shoots of bulbs peeking out from beneath the membrane of the dead earth, a flat surface of hints as to what the Olympic village was going to look like after a year or eighteen months, between the bare, ugly sea and the terrorized leftovers of what remained of Pueblo Nuevo, of that Pueblo which had been 'Nuevo' when the city's bourgeoisie laid out their factories down by the sea, and when they decided to have their manpower living near at hand, despite the risk that the close proximity of the workers to the factories might mean that the bosses would be landed with a Long March, from Pueblo

Nuevo to Icaria, and all Barcelona would become Icaria, and the whole world too.

Lebrun was in favour of getting out and walking for a while, to get a closer view of the building work that was continuing through the night, under floodlights that made it look like the aftermath of some air-raid. What they saw before them could have been either Dresden or Brasilia — a landscape of ruins or foundations, threaded through by unfinished roads which appeared to lead nowhere.

'Imagine how it would be if all this were to be halted right here and now! What a wonderful idea, an unfinished Olympic Village!'

There were signs around proclaiming that the contractors for the construction work were Nueva Icaria Ltd, and this prompted Lebrun to laugh.

'Can you imagine it — one of these days, phalansteries being built by limited companies! Or maybe that's the only way of building phalansteries. Icaria, constructed by limited companies, with financial assistance from the European Community and probably the IMF as well. How about this for an idea — now that communism has gone down the drain, why not convert its dream into a Disneyland theme park for the new bourgeoisie? Carvalho, what do you reckon to the idea of setting up a Disneyland which is a model of the perfect communist city, without the disasters of the communist cities whose collapse we have just witnessed?'

Carvalho called to mind the faces of communists he had known and he had a sudden desire to treat Lebrun to a kick in the balls. But by now they were back in the taxi, in the labyrinth that was Pueblo Nuevo. All of a sudden the landscape began to proletarianize itself, and Lebrun began to show interest in the surroundings. Pueblo Nuevo offered a collage of a community — fishermen and industrial workers, factories and warehouses.

'What did they used to make here?'

'Everything, I think. Textiles, oil presses, antimony, wine, pig-skins for sausages . . .'

'Pig-skins for sausages . . .' intoned Lebrun, as if it had been a poem. The cab-driver requested a degree of exactitude on the kind of square they were looking for, and when Claire explained about the eating house and its fast-food menu, the driver at least seemed to know where they were going. A square in retreat, almost entirely occupied by ombus trees that had been decimated by the autumn, ancient industrial warehouses and long-dead commercial concerns. On the corner stood the bar, and it had a definite flavour of camembert and pan con tomate: the Restaurant Els Pescadors. Claire was still leading the way, but as she went to push the door open, Lebrun restrained her for a moment.

'Tell me, darling, I'd like to know exactly what we're expecting to find here. I would say that's the least I could expect, after all my efforts in bringing you to this city.'

'So was I the only one with an interest in finding Alekos?'

Lebrun met her gaze, and recovered his smile. He let her go on ahead, and after they had scanned the occupied tables and not found what they were looking for, they went to sit at one of the antique marble tables, with its curly cast-iron supports, and were rather put out to hear the owner inquire: 'What would you like to eat?'

'Bring us some well-chilled *cava* and some very thinly sliced ham,' Carvalho asked, and Lebrun seemed to wash his hands of involvement in whatever was to follow. When the waiter brought their order, Carvalho got in ahead of Claire's attempts to formulate a question, and took the initiative himself.

'We're looking for a painter, a Greek.'

Claire brought the photo out of her bag and handed it to the waiter.

'We get a lot of people passing through here.'

'All Greeks?'

'We don't interrogate them on their nationality.'

The waiter referred to higher authority, and the man who was evidently the boss of the establishment, probably an ex-progressive who would get a bit part in one of Dotras's shows one day, sized them up from a distance. Although he disappeared behind the counter and appeared to be absorbed in preparing an order, his brain was evidently working on their inquiry, and a couple of times Carvalho caught him glancing over at a table in a corner. At the table was a group of chattering girls and silent men; they were eating and looked as if they had just come out of a fashion show for a bunch of Arab sheikhs. The girls were dressed as houris, in pink and sky-blue costumes, and the men were wearing tuxedos, like something out of an after-shave ad. Finally the restaurant's owner emerged from his trench and went over to the corner table. He leaned over the group, and said something to one of the young women. Every head at the table turned and looked at Carvalho, Claire and Lebrun. The Frenchman pretended not to notice that he was being looked at; Claire assumed an expression of calm expectation; and Carvalho signalled with his eyes that he was aware that they were being observed. The young woman got up and came over to their table. She was very slim, with the kind of supple body that characterizes the world's best models.

'They tell me you're looking for Alekos.'

'Madama Farandouri is trying to find her husband,' Carvalho said, ignoring Claire's sudden gesture of protest. Something approaching complicity and a certain compassion informed the model's smile.

'He doesn't come here so much these days, and I'm not sure which warehouse he actually lives in. All I know is that it's called Skala, and there's a sign on the door to that effect. We know him from seeing him around the place, and sometimes we walk back together, because we work for a fashion photographer who has a studio in one of the old factories. But he goes further on, and he's never taken us back to where he lives. When we've finished eating we'll be going back to the studio, and if you like you can come with us. At least we can show you most of the way.'

Claire rewarded her with the best smile that Carvalho had seen since he first set eyes on her, and as the model returned to her table, her eyes were full of tears, and her lips were murmuring:

'Skala. It must be Alekos. Couldn't be anyone else.'

'What does "Skala" mean?'

'It's the little port of the island of Patmos, the island where Alekos comes from. We were there three summers ago. We did a trip round the island in a little boat. Grikou, Diakofti, and Hora, the grotto where it's said that Saint John wrote the Book of Revelations.'

Lebrun emerged from something that was either somnolence or feigned indifference, and began to recite: 'In the Spirit he carried me away, and there I saw a woman mounted on a scarlet beast which was covered with blasphemous names and had seven heads and ten horns. The woman was clothed in purple and scarlet and bedizened with gold and jewels and pearls. In her hand she held a cup, full of obscenities and the foulness of fornication.'

He relieved Claire of her perplexity by announcing:

'Revelations, chapter seventeen, verse three.'

'It's strange, but Patmos isn't far from the island of Icaria.'

'Have you been to Patmos too, Monsieur Lebrun?'

'I was with Alekos in the summer of 1987.' There was a note of challenge in the looks which Claire and Lebrun exchanged.

'Alekos is your problem.'

'You mean he's not yours?'

Lebrun interrupted his altercation with Claire in order to continue his conversation with Carvalho.

'You should see the island — go and dry out in its barrenness, become one of its dry inhabitants, and then you would understand why Saint John chose to write the Book of Revelations there. Durrell says that Revelations is a poem worthy of Dylan Thomas. Are you familiar with the writings of Dylan Thomas?'

'Don't forget, I don't read. I only burn books.'

'The number seven is cabalistic, and you find it both in the geological make-up of Patmos and in Saint John's poem: seven hills, seven candlesticks, seven stars. There's a crack in the roof of the cave where Saint John is supposed to have lived. They say it was opened by the voice of God when it came down to enter the saint's body, taking possession of him, poetically speaking, for poetry. The voice of God must have been a terrible thing to hear. I visited the cave one day during a storm, and I don't mind telling you I was scared. The wind was howling outside, and inside the cave you could hear the noise of the mountain as if it was rebelling against God's judgement . . . But what you hear is in fact the noise of water, because even though the island is so barren, the Mountain of the Apocalypse is full of secret springs. The monk who accompanied me was so frightened that he was crossing himself every time the wind roared, and I have to say his fear was catching.'

'And Alekos?'

'He was of the opinion that the entire New Testament, including the Apocalypse, was a shady business thought up by Jews and Jewish pre-capitalists. He didn't have that Judeo-Christian guilt complex which is so stifling in me. He was a primal man, and in that cave he actually felt as if he was a force of nature.'

Claire was listening with an air of fascination. Carvalho couldn't tell whether this was to do with Lebrun or with the man of her dreams.

'I was glad when we finally got out of that cave and back to the harbour. That night, Alekos went on a primal binge. He was like a drunken giant. Or maybe a drunken mountain. We were in a taverna which had most of its windows missing, and the sky was full of streaks of brilliant white lightning — I've never seen lightning so white. It looked like searchlights in the sky, or the way you see searchlights in black and white films. I was scared, and when you think that Porto Skala is supposed to be a shelter from the winds, a haven for pirates and sailors in the olden days ... I tell you, it didn't provide much shelter when the wind really blew. But then again, it's probably all a figment of someone's imagination anyway. It's never been proved that Saint John actually wrote the Apocalypse there. Maybe it wasn't even him who wrote it. So why don't we just decide that it was really written by Dylan Thomas?'

'I'd have no objection to that. Why did you go to Patmos with Alekos, then?'

'Tourism. In-depth tourism.'

And he began to laugh. Exaggeratedly, excessively. Then he calmed down and continued his conversation.

'I met Claire's in-laws. Irreproachable. Anthropologically irreproachable, straight out of an engraving by Gustave Doré, or one of Delacroix's paintings of Greeks. They didn't have the melancholic madness of their son, and they were the kind of family who, when you set off on a journey, put twenty francs in your pocket whether you liked it or not, and a good piece of Roquefort in your case so that you don't die of hunger or dysentery en route. Admirably conventional.'

On the model's table there were signs of departure. Claire tensed slightly, and Carvalho had to clear his mind of the queries which had assailed him after Lebrun's last utterances. How did Lebrun come to know so much about the ins and outs of peasant families? Maybe he had learned his aristocratic behaviour from books, and maybe it was from books that he had taken his novelish description of Alekos's family.

The beautiful body of the Corinthian houri gently stirred the air around her as she invited them to follow the troupe of revellers. The houris went in front and their menfolk behind, laughing and jostling beneath the stars of Icaria, followed by Claire, who was walking like a woman obsessed, and then Carvalho, walking like a man obsessed, and finally, bringing up the rear, their princely expert in apocalypses and Greek peasant families. They passed down an imaginary defile. To their left were small, old houses where everything was stone dead or fast asleep, while on the right were warehouses and unidentifiable, half-abandoned buildings in the moonlight, like obstacles that had been put there to stop you seeing the Olympic construction work and the filthy sea, which, at this point, received the major part of what Barcelona's drains had to offer, inadequately filtered by the purifying beds at the sewage works.

They advanced into this obsolete industrial landscape, an array of shapes which the night rendered almost whimsical: triangular rooftops, joined together like Siamese twins, chimneys bent and curved by long-gone heat, iron towers with their rust ennobled by the moonlight, trees peering out from crumbling perimeter walls and proclaiming victory over the world of industry, and obscure plants of various sorts, all awaiting the final implacable assault of the bulldozers. All their procession needed now was an old violinist and a fat Fellini prostitute, Carvalho thought, and he said as much to Claire, but she didn't check her advance until the models stopped and waited for them. The beautiful body had a voice that was rather over-shrill, but this was a minor consideration.

'This is where we work. Another couple of hundred yards down there you'll find an abandoned factory that used to be called . . . something or other . . . I don't remember . . . You'll see some letters, a blue ceramic sign, very pretty, a bit broken and with some of the letters missing, and that's why I don't remember . . . But somebody has painted the word "Skala" up on the wall, next to the door. You should find Alekos there.'

She had included them all in this 'you', but her eyes were fixed on Claire and were expressing both complicity and compassion. In exchange she received one of Claire's prettiest smiles and a slight bow of Lebrun's head. The revellers disappeared behind an iron door which opened with a screech of protest, like the best doors in the best Dracula films, and the three adventurers were left alone on a street which had long since been abandoned to rats and cats. Claire was the first to get to the door, and she raised one hand as if to caress each of the letters that made up the word Skala. But the gentleness of her gesture was countered by the marked annoyance expressed by her body when she found that the door was locked. The three of them were stuck there, outside the gates of the forbidden city that they had so eagerly sought. The perimeter walls were high, and the door showed no sign of shifting.

'It's very definitely locked.'

'From inside?'

'Impossible to say.'

Claire was just about to start shouting Alekos's name

and kicking at the door impatiently, when Lebrun took her by the arm.

'Calm down. Maybe they don't want to be found. There must be a simpler way. The important thing is to find out how we get into this place. Our model friends would probably know. Let's go back, and we can ask them, and then come back.'

'You two go, I'm staying here.'

'I don't think it'd be very sensible for you to stay here on your own.'

'I can take care of myself.'

'We shouldn't be more than ten minutes. We'll go straight down and straight back, and hopefully by then we'll have found the answer.'

'He's inside. I have this feeling that he's inside, that he's locked himself in.'

In the end she decided to follow them, and once again found herself confronting a labyrinth of avenues over which factory buildings cast lunar shadows. Rusting abandoned railway wagons; cables hanging down from who knows where; broken office furniture lying around in asbestos-roofed sheds, an old Citroën stripped of its wheels and its engine; cardboard boxes piled high in some kind of architectonic order, and which, having been bleached over time, were now converted into a soft white mountain. Off in the distance the sound of a rock concert held out a welcome if you could only pick your way out of this derelict landscape, with its rusting rails interspersed with yellow flowers. Carvalho led the way and overcame the resistance of a small galvanized door to usher his companions into one of the factories. In the light of floodlights that were hanging from the ceiling a group of girls was attempting a ballet which was presumably modern, because they moved as if they were making a mockery of their own bodies, and the music sounded like somebody going through a steel cable with a handsaw. Their movements were supervised by a small fat woman who showed great elasticity as she bent back and forth and showed the dancers what they were doing wrong. No sign of the advertising models, though, and no chance of enquiring as to their whereabouts until the dance director finally got tired of torturing herself and announced a five-minute break. At this point she noticed their presence and began waving her hands around. The hands said 'No, no', and then found their way to her face.

'I warned you, no photographs in here! It's all too unrehearsed.'

'We're not here to take pictures. We're looking for a group of models,' said Carvalho.

'A group of models! And then you'll pop up and start taking photos when I least expect it . . .!'

'No, really, we're looking for a group of models. Although in fact we don't necessarily need to find them. We're actually looking for a Greek.'

'One minute you're looking for models, and now it's a Greek . . .'

'I admire your work, but I assure you I'm not not a photographer. It's true what I told you — we're looking for some models who seem to have some idea of how we can find this Greek. A few yards down road, there's another abandoned factory, just like this one, and it's possible that our friend is in there, but the door's locked, probably from the inside; you wouldn't happen to know if there's any way of getting in, would you? If there's a side door, or a way through from one of the other factories?'

'I hardly ever leave these four walls, and I don't know any Greeks either. The models you're talking about go there sometimes. But they're nothing to do with me, and I . . . Hey! What are you doing?!'

A secret logic had prompted Claire to take a small camera from her bag, and to destroy the choreographer's fragile psychological equilibrium with a flash which went off like a provocation. Lebrun laughed uproariously, and Claire honoured the indignant woman with one of her most enchanting smiles.

'*I said no photography!*'

She tried to summon up support from her dancers, but they were just standing and watching, overcome by early morning tiredness.

'You see — I can't drop my guard for a moment. Get out of here!'

Once outside, Claire appeared relaxed, as if her forbidden photography had freed her from the night's anxieties, and Lebrun's hilarity continued until they were out of the building and had regained the labyrinth of alleys outside.

'That was brilliant. Why on earth did you do it?'

Now it was her turn to be reduced to tears of helpless laughter, and Carvalho watched this concert of mirth which was interrupted now and then by Lebrun as he mimicked the choreographer's voice banning them from taking photographs.

' "No photographs!" she said, and Claire went . . . click . . .!'

Alekos seemed momentarily to have been forgotten, and the couple re-entered the labyrinth with their curiosity renewed, to see what other monsters the night might throw up, in the hope that they might be as entertaining as the one they had just vanquished.

'In the quest for the Holy Grail, perilous were the trials through which the knight Percival had to pass!' Lebrun declaimed, with a renewed energy that took him towards a rectangle of light thrown by the open door of another building.

'This city doesn't sleep. It's fascinating — it seems to sleep, but it doesn't. It's extraordinary. Who would ever imagine that big old buildings like these could be all full of magicians? Don't you find it fascinating, Carvalho? Do you know this area well? I find it wonderful!'

'Vagrants. All these people are vagrants, in a city that is on the point of being destroyed.'

'The models too?'

'The models too. Vagrants and vagabonds.'

'It's possible that you're right. After all, maybe we're all vagrants. Society could be divided into yuppies and vagrants.'

'At this time of night I'm not usually much in the mood for talking. Let's find the Greek and get it over with.'

'Let's do it.'

The open door led to a system of small rooms with

high ceilings, which then issued into a large hall-like space. In this space a giant sculpture was taking shape, which looked to Carvalho as if it was an artichoke, even though something in him was unwilling to admit that this could actually be the case. Next to this bizarre vegetable rose a metal scaffold, and perched on the top was a young man who at that moment was more intent on examining them than on pursuing his bizarre work of art.

'Is it an artichoke?' Carvalho inquired.

'An artichoke. Indeed it is.'

Despite the distance, he was sure that he had seen the face before. That face belonged to someone fairly well-known around town. Lebrun was walking round the artichoke, studying it, and Claire had once again pulled out her camera. She waved it at the man up on his perch.

'Fire away, sister, fire away. Photograph as much as you like. The thing's going to be a public sculpture in the end . . .'

'This thing . . . a public sculpture?'

'I just made it; whether or not they decide to exhibit it is up to them.'

The sculptor began a slow descent, and when he reached ground level he confirmed what Carvalho had suspected, that he was one of the city's more fashionable artists, even though he couldn't actually remember his name. Marcial, or Marisco . . . something like that.

'For the Olympics?'

'No. It was commissioned by the College of Humanities, for a conference. They wanted a monument to relative truth.'

'An artichoke?'

'An artichoke,' the artist confirmed, whereupon he began to examine his creation with eyes that looked strained, either because of the strength of the overhead light, or because he hadn't been sleeping.

'The artichoke is a lovely plant. You keep taking leaves off her, and she just carries on and on until there's nothing left. I would love to have been God, to have designed things like that. What tribe are you all from? You look like you've popped out of a twenty-year-old copy of *Vogue*, and your two friends look as if they've come out of some movie.'

Claire laughed, and the artist liked the way she laughed.

'We're looking for a Greek by name of Alekos.'

'You look a bit like a cop to me. Are you a cop?'

'No. I'm Anselm the First, a friend of the family.'

'I have a painter friend who's crazy about poetry, and he knows a poem about someone called Anselm the First.'

'I'm sure it can't have been me.'

'How does it go, the poem?' Claire asked him.

'I've got an appalling accent when I recite.'

'I'm sure it will be enchanting.'

'You're not from round here. You've got a foreign accent. Anyway, I'll recite the poem. It's a beauty. A surrealist poem of the sort that cuts your brain open with a razor.

This hunchback who is putting himself through
     the keyhole
Is sticking needles in my eyes
Is playing with your buttocks, your breasts
Is pissing in a book of Mao.
It seems to be Volume Two
He eats a painted pheasant
He belches and regathers the air with his hand
While he defecates slowly, gently
On your chocolate mousse:
     It's Anselm the First.
Do you remember?
How could you not?
Manolo has told me so much about you.'

Carvalho was considering the possibility of asking him
for the title of the book, just in case one day it came
sufficiently close to hand to be consigned to his
everlasting bonfire. But he was disturbed by the
obvious interest that Claire was showing for this
sculptor of artichokes, whom the detective had now
identified as the creator of the strange shellfish erected
at the Moll de la Fusta, the smiling prawn which
towered over the little bars like a monster out of some
Japanese film where the monsters are all conscious of
being papier mâché.

'I was asking you about this Greek ...'

'I know there's a Greek who hangs around here
somewhere, but I can't tell you where. He's a painter, or
at least he was.'

'Alekos. He's called Alekos?' said Claire, by way of informing but also asking.

'Yes, I think he's still called Alekos.'

'What do you mean, *still* called Alekos?'

'Is this Greek someone special to you?'

'I'm more or less his wife.'

'You're bound to find him in an abandoned factory further down this street. Nobody uses it, because it's hardly even got a roof, but there's still a few corners where a person can hide away.'

'The factory's all shut up, and we think that Alekos is probably still inside.'

'If he is inside, he won't be on his own. He always goes around with another Greek.'

'Is he called Mitia? I mean — Dimitrios.' Lebrun intervened.

'I believe so.'

Carvalho turned to Lebrun.

'This is new. How many Greeks are we actually looking for?'

'Two,' Lebrun replied, looking him in the eye. Carvalho turned back to the artist.

'Is there some way of getting into the factory from round the back?'

The sculptor was obviously considering Carvalho himself more than his question.

'Maybe you're not a cop, but you ask questions like a cop. I'm afraid I can't tell you. My artichoke awaits me. I have to hand it over before the end of the month, and I'm not happy with this casting. I've had it brought here because this was the place where I worked out its dimensions with the scale model. There's definitely something about it that I don't like.' And he went to climb back up his scaffold. Carvalho was the one who was most impatient to leave. The other two seemed to have lost some of their pressing interest in the Greek, particularly Lebrun, who strolled round the giant artichoke a couple more times as if he was trying to help the artist to identify the reason for his visual dislike.

'Maybe the stalk's too chunky.'

'It has to be chunky, because otherwise the wind will blow it over and I'll have to put cables on it, which I don't want to do. I had to put cables on the prawn on the Moll de la Fusta.'

He finally managed to get Claire and Lebrun to follow him, although the Frenchman was still looking back at the artichoke, obviously impressed by its volume and its hidden meanings which he was busy deciphering. When he finally lost sight of it, Lebrun rubbed his hands and proclaimed:

'We should go through every shed in this place, inch by inch. It's full of lunatics, Carvalho. We should lift the roofs of places like these on the outskirts of cities, these no-man's lands, and I suspect we'd find a whole army of marginalized creativity.'

'Don't go deluding yourself that this is a new continent. It isn't, it's just an island that's sinking.'

'Alekos,' said Claire, in a strangled voice. Carvalho looked round to see if there was anything to indicate the man's presence, but they were simply back on the main path of the labyrinth, and Claire had just re-connected with the purpose of their quest.

'We have to find that model again. She seemed to have the best idea about how to find Alekos.'

'We should pick the warehouse with the most light coming from it. Models always work with the best light,' Lebrun suggested, and Carvalho concurred.

There were still three sheds to be explored, and the choice seemed simple. One was completely dark; another was lit by a feeble yellow light; and from the third shone the brilliant blue of an artificial, man-made sky. They headed towards it. It turned out to be an enormous warehouse. They crossed the threshold through the invisible wall which separates us from the dimension of the unknown. They found themselves in the midst of an Arab market, where the houris were dancing around three men in tuxedos, following the instructions of a chubby man perched on the platform of a camera dolly.

'Maribel, could you get your tits up a bit, love.'

'Leave me alone, will you . . . ?'

'Can someone get something to stack Maribel with? By this time of night we should be finished! And you, Pepe, OK, you're no Fred Astaire, but do you think you could manage your tap-dancing without having to look at the floor . . . It looks like you're stamping on cockroaches. Has anybody killed that family of rats in the corner over there? I don't want to see them, even dead. Now, the lighting effects on the big bottle . . . We're going to have to finish in forty-eight hours what we haven't been able to do so far in two weeks. How goes with the tits, Maribel?'

'I told you, I haven't got any.'

'Well go and have an operation, then, and get yourself something chunky up top. Now, Paquita, those tits . . . Give Maribel something a bit decent. What are you three doing in the studio?'

Like God almighty from up on his perch he had spotted the three new arrivals.

'Ha! Spies! Here doing commercial espionage, eh? What agency are you from?'

'We're doing a publicity short for artificial dandruff.'

At first the director was irritated by Carvalho's smart-Alec reply, but then he laughed and relaxed. Everybody in the place was looking at them, and the titless Maribel came over to greet them. She was the guide they had met in the restaurant.

'They're my friends.'

'Well give them a big hello from all of us and let's get back to bloody work.'

Maribel took them across to an open space between the cameras.

'What's the matter?'

'The warehouse is all locked up, either from the outside or from the inside. If he's not there, where else could he be?'

'He must be there.'

She said it as if Alekos couldn't possibly be anywhere else. She obviously understood how important all this was for Claire, and set about putting her more fully in the picture.

'I don't want to alarm you, but he's in pretty bad shape. They took him to hospital, and he just upped and left because he reckoned he'd never get out of the place alive. He's living with his friend in that warehouse that we sent you to. They've probably barred the door from the inside. The empty factories round here are a waste land . . . it's the law of the jungle there . . .'

'Will they open if we shout?'

'I don't think they'd hear you. They live at the other end of the building. You could try something else, though. Go in through the warehouse next door . . . If you want to wait while we finish this take, I can show you how to get in.'

She ran back to the set, and allowed her bosom to be filled out by señora Paquita. One of the director's production assistants gave the final instructions, and the director's voice boomed out from the heavens, 'Roll sound . . . Roll camera . . .' Carvalho waited, fascinated, in the hope that something exciting was about to happen, but all that happened was that the houris sprayed scent on their handsome male counterparts, and they in turn went tap-dancing across the set, while behind them a giant bottle of men's *eau de toilette* rose into view.

'Cut! That's a lot better. One more take, and that'll do. You, Ingrid, when you spray your partner with the cologne, try and give it a bit of charm, would you?'

'He's such a bastard, though.'

'That fact is of no interest to our sponsor.'

'Be mine tonight, darling,' proclaimed the injured party, as he went and tried to kiss a tall skinny blonde. The director was drinking Coke straight from a litre bottle which he then placed carefully on the platform so as not to tip over its ambrosiac contents. He distributed instructions and words of encouragement to all and sundry, and they did another take. As far as Carvalho could see it was exactly the same as the one before, but the director was enthusiastic about the result.

'At last! It was an effort, but we did it!'

The unity of the group broke up, under the pressure of tiredness and a strong desire to go home to bed. Maribel put a light coat on, on top of her houri costume, and ran over to the new arrivals, telling them to follow her. They went out into the dead of night. Claire tried to keep up with the woman as she tripped along in her high-heels, in order to ask her more questions about the state of Alekos's health.

'To be honest, I don't really know, and I'd rather not know. He was a very free and easy sort of person, but all of a sudden he started going downhill. I don't want to alarm you, but you should prepare yourself for a shock.'

They emerged from the labyrinth into the street where rats and cats ruled the roost. The model opened the door of the warehouse next to Skala, and they went in to find themselves in what had once been a store-house for building materials. She took them over to a wall on the left and pointed to what appeared to be a set of steps made from broken paving stones.

'If you climb up there, you'll get to the top of the wall, and it should be easy to jump over because there's a pile of rubbish on the other side. The gentleman might find it a bit of an effort, though.'

So saying she gestured towards Carvalho, and the

irony in her tone was too late to pre-empt a snappy response from the detective.

'People haven't started giving up their seats to me on buses yet.'

'I wasn't meaning to be rude.'

'Aren't you coming as well?' Lebrun asked.

'I'm afraid I can't. I don't have my car here, and my friends are waiting for me. But from now on you should find it easy. Take your time as you're looking. It's a big place and I think they like to hide away.'

She kissed Claire on the cheek, and allowed herself to be held for a moment.

'Is he really that ill?'

'I don't know. The last time I saw him he seemed really poorly. In fact he hasn't been to the bar on the square for days now, and Mitia is very evasive, as if he'd rather not talk to anyone.'

She blew Carvalho and Lebrun a kiss, and went off to where she'd come from, a tinkling doll swallowed up by the night. Lebrun appeared nervous about the gymnastic aspect of their expedition.

'You really want to do this now, Claire?'

'What do you suggest otherwise?'

'Why not early tomorrow morning? If you ask me, this is macabre. There's not a light in the place. How are we supposed to find him? By touch?'

'I've got a torch with me,' said Carvalho.

'I'd carry on even if we didn't have a torch. I've waited for this moment for months. I need to get to the end of all this, don't you understand? And I think maybe you need to get it over too?'

'OK ... Let's go.'

Claire held Lebrun back for a moment, hanging onto his sleeve.

'You say nothing, and you do nothing ... Understood? We do everything as agreed.'

'Everything?'

'Everything.'

Now they were looking at Carvalho as if he was somehow in the way, but they appreciated the presence of the torch in his hand, and resigned themselves to the fact that he was coming along. Claire was the first to climb up and peer over into the yard of the warehouse next door.

'It doesn't look so easy from here,' she warned. 'I think you or señor Carvalho should jump first.'

The two men joined her on top, and Carvalho's torch revealed an eighteen-foot drop, which was unlikely to be softened much by the pile of cardboard boxes which lay at the bottom.

'I'm fairly supple,' Lebrun announced. He got astride the top of the wall, held on firmly with both hands, and allowed his body to drop over the other side, searching with his toes for something to support him before he jumped. Finally he found a bit of a ledge and launched himself into space. Carvalho's torch found him sitting on the ground surrounded by cardboard boxes. If he had hurt himself there was no sign of it on his impassive features.

'Your turn, now, Carvalho,' said Lebrun, and Carvalho went through the same routine. The wall was made of hard sandstone which skinned the palms of his hands. His hands hurt, and since it felt like he'd pulled a muscle or two in his armpits he finally let go more in order to escape the pain than to complete the logical order of his actions. Lebrun half caught him as he fell and deadened the weight of his fall, whereupon Carvalho found himself bandy-legged and somewhat shaken on top of an inadequate cushion of rotting cardboard boxes. He straightened up, his body aching all over, and stood next to Lebrun in order to help catch Claire. His torch illuminated her shapely, bare legs, protruding beneath the bell of her skirt. When she jumped it was like a parachute falling into the four arms of the men below. Carvalho had never held her close, and was happy to feel the impact of that firm flesh and catch the early-morning country smell of the woman. He availed himself of this opportunity to feel for himself, to feel the substance of her in his arms, in a functional embrace that was shared with Lebrun. The Frenchman detached himself as soon as Claire was safely down. Carvalho didn't, and this prompted Claire to look him straight in the eye. The look was neither of irony nor of promise. Rather of surprise, and of friendly dissuasion. Then they set off, and scrambled down the mound of cardboard. The woman went first, and led them into a huge shed which occupied virtually the whole of the site. Carvalho went on ahead, wielding his torch and revealing the innards of this industrial cathedral which, in the darkness, had all the mystery of some great Gothic church. The building was a single unit, divided into various sections, and they found themselves going through spaces dedicated to industrial purposes whose nature they could only guess at. As they searched, each of them felt that slowly but surely the moment of truth was near. They picked their way among soiled bales of cloth, cotton waste, balls of string, useless account books, calendars from the early nineteen-sixties, metal lamps with no bulbs in, tangled electric cables, filthy demijohns covered in dust and cobwebs, and small furtive creatures scurrying into the darkest corners of the place. The beam of Carvalho's torch was like a fountain pen writing an inventory of all this ruin and wreckage. All of a sudden they found themselves under a large central nave from the roof of which hung pulleys and hoists for mysterious industrial processes that were long since dead and gone.

'It's like finding your way into some great pyramid of industrial society,' Lebrun mused, but neither Claire nor Carvalho chose to examine this proposition further. From the centre of the shed, Carvalho's torch picked out in detail every corner of the floor, the walls, and the metal framework of the roof. Not a sign of anyone or anything, but there were signs of other areas to explore before their search was over. They went through a small door and arrived at the bottom of a staircase which led up to a kind of attic. It was at the foot of this staircase that Claire called out for the first time.

'Alekos!'

The two men stood still, for fear that their movements might obstruct the possibility of an eventual reply. They thought they heard sounds of life up under the roof, but there wasn't enough light to be able to check, and they weren't in the mood to talk and share their impressions. Carvalho began to climb the stairs, with his torch at the ready, and they arrived at a door barricaded from behind with a lump of wood.

'Alekos!' Claire called again, but there was no reply, and this time not even a hint of a sign of life. Carvalho put his shoulder to the door, and the sound of cracking, splintering wood suddenly disturbed the sedimented silences of the enormous space below. When the last echoes finally ebbed and they were ready to go on, they saw that there was a corridor on the other side of the open rectangle, and from the end they heard a half choked murmur that signalled either fear or caution. The area of light cast by Carvalho's torch was suddenly filled by Claire, who wanted to be the first to reach the end of their adventure. Carvalho had to point the torch downwards to illuminate her path from behind. The corridor led to a point where there were several possible paths that they could take, but the stifled noises seemed to be coming from the right. Claire followed the noises, arriving finally at a room into which a high window let in the light of a moon which had momentarily overcome the resistance of the clouds. In the moonlight they saw two figures huddled against the wall. The torch cornered them for just sufficient time to describe them, surprise them, terrify them, and then have pity on them. There was the man from the photograph, or what was left of him, and next to him a young man who had been mistreated by circumstances that remained unfathomable. Alekos was a living skeleton, and from his skull-like face emerged two eyes that seemed all the larger because of the smallness of the rest of his decimated frame. His lips murmured the names of Claire and Georges, asking was it really them, as if it could have been anyone else ... At his side, the younger man smiled and seemed somehow impatient. As if he had been waiting for this moment for a long time, as if it somehow promised a moment of liberation.

'Alekos,' said Claire.

'Mitia,' said Lebrun.

It was at this point that Carvalho realized that the woman and Lebrun were not looking for the same person. However, it was not his job now to understand this encounter, but only to facilitate it, by keeping the light focused on the objects of their attention. Claire went forward and covered Alekos's body with hers as he sat up, resting on one elbow. The light of the torch played with the woman's silhouette as she leaned over to be the only one who could hear what was coming from Alekos's lips. Mitia, Lebrun and Carvalho had turned into mute bystanders, and this stifled conversation proceeded for several minutes, with Claire stroking the fallen man's face as if she was discovering it for the first time. None of the men would have dared to try to venture into this forbidden territory of affection. After a while she turned round, obviously irritated by the crude light of the torch. Carvalho switched it off, muttering an apology that was heard only by himself and perhaps also by Lebrun, who was observing the scene and who seemed overcome by a sudden and total depression. There they stood for minutes on end, not moving, not saying a word, and respecting the canopy of time and silence which enveloped the conversation between Claire and the man of her life. Finally Claire rose to her feet and stood for a few seconds, lost in thought. Then she turned round, caressed Alekos's face once more, and turned back to Lebrun and Carvalho. She took Lebrun aside into a dark corner, where they conversed in subdued terms. There was as much silence as words in their conversation, and after a while she hugged Lebrun, asked him for something — perhaps for understanding — and having concluded their negotiations they rejoined Carvalho. It was Claire who took the initiative.

'We're going to stay here for a while.'

'I can wait for you outside, for as long as necessary.'

'No, you leave. We're staying here.'

It was an order, and brusquely delivered at that. Lebrun took Carvalho by the arm and ushered him out of the room. When they reached the end of the corridor, the Frenchman said:

'I'm sorry, this is all terribly emotional for her. We're very grateful to you. You've done everything we asked you to do, and more. Very rapidly, too, remarkably rapidly, in fact.'

'It was relatively simple. If you want to find vagrants, you go and look among vagrants.'

'We don't want to trouble you more than necessary. Your job is done now. From now on it's up to us.'

'I see.'

'I'll see you to the exit.'

'I can find it on my own.'

But he sensed that the Frenchman needed to be sure

that he had actually left, so he allowed himself to be shown out, with the intention of then leaving them the torch for when they decided to leave the place. Lebrun followed him out of the building, having first removed the wooden bar that blocked the main entrance and prevented access from the outside.

'You can keep the torch. You'll need it when you leave here. You can give it back when you come in to settle your bill.'

'I'll include the price of the torch in the bill. I'll be posting you a cheque. This is probably the last time we'll see each other.'

At this Carvalho was disconcerted, and he felt a sudden pain in his chest.

It wasn't his resentment at being left in the dark about the outcome of the case; it was the fact that he knew he wasn't going to be seeing Claire again.

'Well, maybe we'll need to . . .'

'You'll have no reason to complain about the cheque. Goodbye, señor Carvalho.'

He offered Carvalho the same hand that was ushering him out. Carvalho shook it in return, and when he was on his own again he reproached himself for the degree of dependency that he had shown at the last moment. He felt like some native kid who had fallen in love with two French tourists and had then been suddenly demoted from his status of guide to the white man. There are moments in the life of a sensitive adolescent which remain buried and hidden in the spirit and come out when you least expect them, Carvalho told himself. He suddenly felt the need for a

large glass of whisky and the saving grace of clean
sheets — his sheets, to be precise, which understood the
needs and weaknesses of his body. He walked on faster
until he arrived at the civilized part of Pueblo Nuevo,
and found a taxi. He couldn't decide whether to tell the
driver to take him to where he'd left his car parked, or
straight home to Vallvidrera. His need for sheets, sleep
and whisky was urgent, however, so he plumped for the
second option, and when he arrived home he filled the
tub with hot water and sank himself into a bath that
would wash away all the night's mysteries, the cobwebs
and the premonitions of death. Death. The letters of the
word seemed to fall apart, and the D danced around in
his brain as he plunged his head under the soapy water.
Finally he emerged from beneath the waves, and felt as
if he had finally achieved a kind of total cleanliness,
both inside and out. And in place of the gloomy letter D
in his mind's eye, there was the smiling face of Claire,
those ironic, sensual lips, the peachy texture of her skin,
her honey-coloured hair, and once again he had to tell
himself that the exception confirmed the rule as
regards his life, his work, his Biscuter, his Charo, and
poor Bromide, now dead as a doornail. He cast an eye
around the four corners of his apartment, and was glad
to note the disappearance of the world of ruins that he
had traversed that night. There was, however, something still bothering his brain: the way that Claire had
greeted the one man and Lebrun had greeted the other.

'Alekos,' she said.

'Mitia,' he said.

Why? What was the reason? What were they doing

there, in the shadows, now? What words were passing
between them? What new story were they now cons-
tructing between those ruined walls, towards some
possible future? It took a good three whiskies before he
felt relaxed and able to surrender himself to sleep. His
sheets helped. They were freshly changed, and just
what he needed to send him off into a sleep that was
deep, but at the same time disturbed.

When he woke it was because he felt he needed to call Charo and let her know that he needed her, in the same way that any husband rediscovers the value of his wife when he comes unstuck in affairs of the heart, whether real or imagined. The need he felt was an extension of his dream, which had been all about their search the night before. Charo had turned up as the fourth member of their expedition, although Claire hadn't known who she was, and Carvalho had chosen to ignore her. But Charo had persevered in trying to make her presence felt. She kept chipping in, trying to make herself useful. She would offer suggestions as to the best way to find Alekos, and she would voice her approval of what she considered the most constructive proposals. Every now and then Lebrun would strike up conversation with her, and while Charo was happy to be the object of his attention, she had no eyes for him, but only for Carvalho, in the hope that he would acknowledge her presence. Stubbornly he spent his whole dream refusing to allow Charo to go along with them and replying to her observations as if they had been made by Claire or Lebrun, or by himself. However, when they were on the way back from their adventure, through a landscape of stylized rubbish, Charo came up to him and started talking, talking, talking incessantly, offering a forgettable account of everything that had happened. She seemed to be describing the day's events, but what was Charo really saying in his dream? Something about money, because all of a sudden he began to worry about the cheque? Or maybe about visibility, because Charo and the cheque were then replaced by the image of his torch? He hated parting with personal possessions — to such an extent that he never threw anything away, even when it had long outlived its usefulness. Did he perhaps do the same thing with people? That torch had lived some excellent moments in the bottom of his jacket pocket. Hundreds and hundreds of times it had died, with its batteries exhausted, and hundreds and hundreds of times he had brought it back to life, putting in fresh batteries and switching it on to check if it was working, whereupon it would send out a signal of its resurrection, with the self-satisfaction shown by all objects when they work properly. He imagined that the poor thing had been dumped somewhere in that desolate landscape that was waiting for the pickaxe and the bulldozer which were going to tear open the flesh of old Barcelona and bury a good part of his best and worst memories. Probably Claire and Lebrun had just thrown it away on a rubbish heap. They wouldn't even have given his torch a decent last resting place. What would his pathetic little torch have meant to them? Carvalho could still feel in his hand the weight, the texture and the feel of his torch. Ever since he'd left the warehouse, the torch had watched the progress of that strange procession and had waited patiently for Carvalho to come back and save it, to restore the meaning of its life. The torch deserved a better fate than that. He was annoyed with himself for having left it so callously in the hands of Lebrun — mainly because he had left it out of the egotism of a lover who wanted to leave something of his close to Claire, and so prolong his presence there with her.

Caught undecided between the choice of ringing Charo, and doing absolutely anything but that, he opted for the latter. He trailed round the house, and then round the garden, trying to lessen the weight of lost and absent friends on his mind. He remembered that he'd left his car somewhere else, and he was absolutely not in the mood for going down to Barcelona to face up to the reality of the outcome of the case of the lost Greek, or the urgency of the case of the nymphomaniac señorita Brando. He rang the office. Biscuter informed him that on the office desk there was an envelope waiting, an envelope which had the Avenida Palace Hotel as the return address, and a hasty scrawl to indicate that the sender had been Georges Lebrun.

'Open it.'

A cheque for two hundred and fifty thousand pesetas. Not bad for two days' work. He had to admit that the art of generosity had not died. Or perhaps it was simply the efficacy of Lebrun's guilty conscience. Only Lebrun's? Two hundred and fifty thousand pesetas for two days' work, with nothing worse to show for it than the palms of his hands grazed, an ache in his armpits, and a slight pain in the heart every time he thought of Claire. He would invite Charo out for lunch and for a film. Whatever she fancied. He would choose the restaurant, and she could choose the film. Once the initial storm had passed, Charo would not be very demanding, nor would she expect explanations for why he had forgotten her for days on end, without even the courtesy of a phone call. She would realize that he'd been under the influence of something — probably a woman. But she would enjoy the meal and the film, and the fact of having his company again. She would feign fears and happiness on top of a sadness and a fear that were all too real, and would then kiss Carvalho when the occasion offered itself, and ask for his imaginary protection. Or perhaps not so imaginary. However, the unseen malaise continued unabated, and Carvalho went back to hide in the solitude of his house, there, up on the heights, his brain full of the broken images of a city, of this city, of his city, and of all its strange visitors. And the Greek. Or rather, the Greeks.

'Alekos,' Claire had said.

'Mitia,' Lebrun had said.

In his mind's eye he still saw the pair of them, at the end of the labyrinth, or what had seemed to be the end of the labyrinth, picked out in the light of his torch. No, he wouldn't ring Charo for the moment. But he needed to talk with someone, so he rang his neighbour the agent Fuster, in the hopes of finding him at home. He wasn't. But he was at his office, and was as surprised as

Charo might have been at having suddenly been remembered by Carvalho.

'Are you ill?'

'My body is asking me to cook something, and to eat what I've cooked with somebody who will appreciate it.'

'That's what I'm here for.'

'Come round for supper. Give me all day so I can prepare something complicated, plan it, go out and get what I need, and push myself to the limit.'

'I have to choose between the City of Barcelona orchestra, conducted by our mutual neighbour Blanqueras, and the meal that you're going to cook.'

'I wouldn't want to be an instrument of barbarity. I'll wait for you.' 'What would you say to this for starters: a pyramid of fried aubergine, under a thick layer of tomato sauce with anchovies and a poached egg, and sauce hollandaise, and a spoonful of caviar?' This latter question was directed to himself when he saw that in the fridge he still had a fifty-gramme tin of caviar, which would be enough to share out two generous spoonfuls on top of the wondrously marbled poached eggs. He had enough butter for a sauce hollandaise for two, and some frozen prawns which he could use to concoct a seafood stock which would dilute and at the same time flavour the sauce hollandaise. And for the next course? He turned out the frozen reserves from his fridge, and let out a 'Eureka' when he discovered that he still had some flaky pastry which he could use to fill with stuffing. He didn't even need to leave the house; he was virtually self-sufficient, and he was extremely pleased to discover it. He still had two hours before midday, and he used them to make the seafood stock, with the heads of the prawns, the carrots, the remains of a sad-looking piece of celery, some garlic and a leek which looked more like a mummified spring onion. He cooked the various ingredients, mashed them, put them through the blender, added a glass of white wine, and reduced it over a low flame until it took on a cream-like consistency. At the same time he set about preparing the stuffing — some chicken breast, a pig's trotter that had already been cooked and de-boned, the meat from some pork ribs that he had kept for a *cassoulet*, an onion, tomatoes, a head of garlic, a bouquet of aromatic herbs from his garden, some sage, some marjoram and some bay leaves which were a poor recollection of their previous lustrous green selves. For some reason, the dead yellow bay leaves reminded him of his torch. He gave the whole thing a good sousing with cognac, and having given it the flambé treatment he waited for it to cool so that he could take the meat, mince it, add some breadcrumbs with egg and truffle, and put it to one side to use later for the final sauce. Once the stuffing had cooled, he spread the pastry over a marble slab and cut out four rectangles, in the centre of each of which he placed some of the stuffing. This gave him four small packets of future delight. He dipped them in flour, and fried them gently in oil, first making sure that it was not too hot. Gradually these small packages took the form and colour of imitation pigs' trotters. He mixed the resulting juices with what he had kept from when he cooked the meat, and in these juices he gently fried the vegetables, added the meat stock, plus white wine and cognac, all of which he then put through the blender and thus achieved a thick sauce which was destined to be the dark pool in which the four envelopes would stand with the precision of a musical quartet. That was the second course more or less completed. The aubergines would be dusted with flour and fried, so that they were ready to provide the base of the pyramid. Then he would add the tomato sauce, the caviare from its tin, and on top would go the poached eggs and the sea-food sauce hollandaise just at the moment when the music-loving agent was due to arrive. But it was still only seven o'clock in the evening. Why not try a dessert? He was particularly conscious of Fuster's criticism of his disdain for desserts, which the agent claimed was the result of an underdeveloped gastronomic *education sentimentale*, made up of single dishes, or of longings for unobtainable proteins. He compared the simplicity of the kind of desserts that originate in Italy with the obviousness of the equivalent Spanish desserts; the Italians, by the simple use of flour, almond and egg, contrive to achieve five thousand varieties of sweetness. So he reached for a book — somewhat nervously, because it was a cookery book, one of the few forms of knowledge that he respected as being innocent. The book was the *Talisman of Happiness*, the bible of Italian culinary technique, written by someone who had done so much to popularize Italian cooking — Ada Boni. It had been a present from an Italian-Spanish couple with whom he had had a conversation about cooking and imperialism on a flight from Rome to Barcelona. In the front there was a dedication: 'From señor and señora Corti-Pellejero, to Pepe Carvalho, after a difficult conversation.' It happened that the recipe on the first page he opened coincided with what he had left in his larder. A chestnut soufflé. He had bought the chestnuts as a ritual, or maybe out of nostalgia, in remembrance of the days when his mother used to roast chestnuts in an old frying pan with holes in it, over a fire of the kind of mediocre coal you had immediately after the War, or of coal-nuts made out of coal powder, since their house in the old part of the city still had no electricity and was lit by an acetylene lamp. And along with the chestnuts roasted in her recycled frying pan, there would be *panellet* cakes made from sweet potato, the only sweet raw material that all Spaniards could lay their hands on in those days. My memories won't outlive me, Carvalho thought to himself, and he whistled the tune of a tango, to which he then added improvised words:

> My memories went off with somebody else,
> and left me like a broken toy,
> full of snivelling tears,
> in a corner.

He didn't develop his improvised song as he prepared the base for the soufflé. He cooked the chestnuts, peeled them carefully, put them through the blender, and then tipped the mixture into a small saucepan, where he added butter, a spoonful of cocoa powder, two spoons of sugar, all of which he mixed with a wooden spatula, and continued stirring over a low flame, having first added some drops of vanilla. Once the mixture had been cooked, the time would come for the addition of the beaten egg whites and then, later, the magical growth of the soufflé. He put the mixture into an oven-proof earthenware terrine, which had probably come from Leon or Zamorra, and which he could rely on to retain the heat. Until Fuster arrived and supper was more or less ready to roll, the soufflé would remain in its sleep of the just. By now it was nine o'clock. Why hadn't she tried to contact him at home? Who was 'she'? Charo? Claire? What time would the concert finish? At a decent hour, because a properly balanced culture cannot allow itself to impose imbalances on the rhythms of people's lives. As it turned out, he was asleep by the time Fuster knocked at his door at half past ten. He was dressed in the garb of a lawyer and an agent who had just been to a concert, complete with a silk scarf — or maybe when a scarf is silk it isn't a scarf any more? Fuster listened to Carvalho's proposed menu with a false appearance of imperturbability, and raised an interested eyebrow when Carvalho promised him chestnut soufflé for dessert.

'You're starting to eat well in this house!'

Carvalho placed a pan of water and vinegar on the stove, and when it came to the boil he broke two eggs and tipped their contents into the boiling, vinegary water. He shook the saucepan so that the egg whites would allow the yolk to rise, and after three minutes he used a fish-slice to plunge the eggs into a dish of cold water, where they completed their final transubstantiation into marble. Meanwhile, he used the boiling water in which the eggs had been cooked as a steamer for a little saucepan in to which he put butter, egg yolks, salt, pepper, and half a teaspoon of lemon juice, in order to make the sauce hollandaise. He took it off the flame, added several spoonfuls of the concentrated sea-food stock until he had a taste and texture which he judged appropriate, and he began piling the aubergines onto their respective plates. On top of the aubergines he poured tomato sauce, with anchovies, and, to top it off, the poached eggs, with their edges trimmed back, and then, over the egg, a generous helping of sauce, which filtered into the pyramid; and finally, a spoonful of gelatinous, velvety Iranian caviar. Fuster consumed this baroquery in appropriately baroque style. Each portion that he consumed from his fork was met with ecstatic comments.

'It's a marvellous interplay of textures and tastes: sharp, sweet, salty. And that touch of caviar sets all the rest off wonderfully.'

'You're positively baroque.'

'It's good to eat well.'

He was more critical with the stuffed pigs' trotters, and suggested that perhaps there was something missing.

'Mushrooms, for example.'

However, Carvalho feigned absorption in the state of the soufflé, which was rising and slowly turning golden by the miracle of the beaten egg whites, pushing the timid chestnut purée into false expectations of being able to escape. On the table stood a bottle of Recadero cava *brut natur* and a Valduero red, both bottles now empty, having lost their souls to the stomachs of Fuster and Carvalho. With the chestnut soufflé Carvalho served a Corsican chestnut liqueur which had been hiding in a ceramic bottle in his drinks cabinet for several years.

'The streets of Corcega are full of a curious breed of pigs. They seem to be wild, but in the evening they all come home, stuffed full of chestnuts. I stayed there a few years ago. When I was trying to give up my freedom of travel. One day I'll go back. I find that these days I have to start choosing the places that I want to go back to.'

'What's up this time?'

'What do you mean?'

'Every time you invite me round for supper, it's because you're challenging yourself to cook something, and when you need to cook it's because you're neurotic, obsessed by something that you can't digest.'

'There's a woman that I like too much, and I don't like it when I like a woman too much. The other night I went out with her on a bizarre manhunt, and all of a sudden I found myself wanting her to stay with me for ever — for her to change her life, and me to change mine. It annoys me to feel vulnerable, even if it's only for a day or two. Now she's left or is leaving, and she's left me feeling like an ageing sixteen-year-old with a sense of loss and frustration.'

'The last time I fell in love was about the time they brought out that film with Lee Marvin, Jean Seberg and

Clint Eastwood . . . *Paint Your Wagon*. Twenty years ago, almost. I'd have to conduct an archeological excavation on myself to be able to retrieve that sensation. I remember the film, because it showed a *ménage à trois* in which the old man finally loses out.'

'You weren't that old twenty years ago.'

'I'm about the same age as you. We belong to that class of people who are already forty by the age of eighteen, and who then take forty years to reach the age of forty-one. All a result of having had to grow up too fast after the war.'

'I feel so unsure of myself that I could almost write a poem.'

'And how are things going with Charo?'

'Do me a favour . . .'

'Let's drink something vigorous which will give us back our Superman muscles.'

Carvalho poked around in his shelves of spirits and returned to the dining room with a bottle of Mirambel *eau de vie*. Fuster was just finishing his coffee.

'I say we make way for serious alcohol. This coffee is very good. You've never offered me such good coffee before.'

'I've decided to increase my store of useless knowledge, and the man in the coffee shop in Plaza Buensuceso is giving me lessons; he's made me up a mixture of three-quarters of a pound of first-grade Colombian with a quarter of Dominican.'

'There comes a time when knowledge begins to take up space. You're lucky — you don't read, so you don't have to store up other people's knowledge. You should start reading again, though.'

Carvalho pretended to spit, and Fuster began reciting in French.

' "Cher moi!, le meilleur de mes amis, le plus puissantes de mes protecteurs, et mon souverain le plus direct, agreez l'hommage que je vous fait de ma dissection morale: ce sera tout a la fois un remerciement pour tous les services que vous m'avez rendus, et un encouragement à m'en rendre de nouveaux....!" An amazing man, Restif de la Bretonne! An eighteenth-century writer who knew how to look into his own soul! I'm reading the Pleiade edition. I've bought the whole edition, and I've taken out a subscription for all the forthcoming volumes until the day I die. I've told my various relations that if it turns out that I'm unable to read in my old age, I want them to come and read to me. Do you know Restif de la Bretonne?'

'I can't say I've ever had the pleasure.'

'He wrote a splendid piece. *Monsieur Nicolas*, it's called. I recommend it. He was a very enlightened figure, and a disciplined anarchist in his way. He would make a good reference point for the times that we're living in now. After all, is it possible to be anything other than enlightened, disciplined and anarchist these days? Who would want to be anything else?'

'I would like to learn how to live stripped of my memories, of all my memories, from the earliest to the most recent.'

'The important thing is to get them into proportion. Some people say that in our brains we still retain all the memories of our entire evolution, from when we were fishes, and then amphibians, and then reptiles.'

Fuster continued reciting bits and pieces, each one more obscure than the one before, and Carvalho switched off when the ignoble erudite began declaiming Italian Renaissance poets, including, among others, a poem in Latin, by a certain Fracastoro, about syphilis. As the level of the *eau de vie* in the bottle sank, so the obscurity and arcaneness of Fuster's ramblings increased. In the end, the agent got tired of holding forth, or perhaps he'd just sunk into a mood, and he looked at Carvalho, who was tracing trails of *eau de vie* across the table with his fingers.

'Enric, we hide too much behind words.'

Fuster got up, slightly wobbly on his legs.

'The dinner was exquisite. Positively anthropological. But now I must be off to my lodgings.'

Carvalho did not have the energy to see him to the door. As ever, he had used Fuster as a means of listening to himself, and now he cleared a place for his arms and head on the table which was piled high with the leftovers of their feast and the invisible remnants of their banquet of words. He slept until the muscles in his shoulders served notice that he ought to change position. He poured his body full of cold water, and let it fall like a damp wine-skin onto his bed. He had no hangover when morning broke — 'because everything we drank was good, and everything we said was pointless,' he told himself — and after a quick shower he rang for a taxi. During the steep descent, he found himself wishing he was in his own car, which was so used to the route that it could more or less find its own way down Collcerola, the stretch of hill which was now besieged by the building works for the ring-roads and tunnels that were going to change the coordinates of his city. Arriving in the Ramblas, he decided to catch up with reality, so he bought various newspapers, and even went so far as to read them. *El Periodico* in particular, which had a story about the discovery of a body in Pueblo Nuevo, a foreigner, who had died of an overdose. Carvalho's eyes toyed with this information, and a thought crossed his mind. A foreigner. Dead from an overdose. Pueblo Nuevo. No concrete reference here. No name. Not even initials. He held at arms length the temptation to think too much, but there at the door of the office stood Biscuter, ready to pour out everything he had done the previous two nights, blow by blow.

'Inspector Contreras sent one of his boys round, boss. He wants to see you. I was wondering whether maybe they were after me . . . I thought maybe they had my card marked, boss. For people like that, once they've got you down in those files they keep up their arses, you're a marked man. Do what you like, you can't win . . . And Mister Brando — I mean, señor Brando — is getting very sniffy, boss, and says he wants to end your contract. And then there's Charo, boss, señorita Charo. She says she'll explain everything in a letter.'

'Explain everything about what, Biscuter?'

'Everything that's worth knowing about, that's what señorita Charo said, and she was crying, boss, and generally complaining.'

'What were Contreras's boys after? Why are they breathing down our necks?'

'They said something about a Greek. *The* Greek. I never said a word. Is it true he's dead?'

'It's possible. Ring Mr Brando and tell him I'm on his case, and that I'm hot on the trail. Did no one else ring?'

'No.'

'Have you been here all the time?'

'She hasn't rung.'

So she hadn't rung. Even Biscuter knew what was eating into his soul, and partly because he needed emergency treatment and partly because he needed to put the whole thing behind him, Carvalho picked up the Brando case again. And behind that naked angel impaled on the old man's sex the faces of her father, her mother and the gymnast rose into view, along with the vacant face of her virtuous, biblical brother. It was a good morning for going to see biblical brothers, so he hunted among his notes for the address of José Luis Brando, managing director of Ediciones Brando, S.A.

'He's a traitor; he wants to sell the company to foreign investors,' the father had warned him.

'He has two brains. One in the normal place, and the other in place of a heart,' the mother had warned him.

The premises of the Brando firm were new, and looked as if they'd been designed by a major architect; they had an entrance hall that was big enough to store all the books that Fuster had been able to read in his life, and all the books that Carvalho had managed to burn over the same period. The women in reception

were dressed like air hostesses on board some inter-
planetary space ship, and the glass doors slid to and fro
as though suspended in a gravity-free bubble. On the
walls hung gigantic photographs of authors that the
firm published, their faces looking grainy as a result of
the excessive enlargement of their photographs, and
Carvalho recognized one or two, thanks in part to his
memory, and in part to the services of the mass media.
He also thought he recognized a few who had gone the
way of his cremational fireplace, but he felt not a trace
of remorse for them. When all's said and done, after all,
he had paid good money for their books. The girl who
inquired what he wanted seemed to have some diffi-
culty putting her words together, perhaps because of
an excess of make-up on her face, but the sense of what
she was trying to transmit to him was expressed more
than adequately by the disdain in her look. Señor
Brando was not in. Since Carvalho was unwilling to
accept this verdict, she corrected it. Señor Brando was
in for nobody. Nobody was Carvalho. However, the
intercom gave a different reply when the girl comm-
unicated Carvalho's final gambit.

'There's a gentleman here who says that your sister
has been arrested.'

There followed a brief silence, then finally and
inevitably a 'Show him through'. Carvalho was surprised to find that he felt as if someone or something
had injected a dose of fear into his veins. Ten years
previously, he would have marched straight in behind
his lie, with his body ready to meet any aggression
head-on. Nowadays he was alarmed to find that he

lived a constant contradiction between form and content, as if his body and his spirit were no longer prepared to hold themselves responsible for his muscles, should it ever come to having to deal with other people's violence. 'You're getting old,' he told himself, and this was not the best frame of mind in which to be meeting with a man who was young and athletic in almost every sense of the word. Brando Junior stood at the end of a never-ending salon, behind a desk that was three times more expensive than that of his father. On the wall hung photographs of various other people who Carvalho deduced were also Brandos, since there were two old photographs which preceded a fairly recent photograph of the first Brando he had met. In other words it was a family concern, now being run by the heir apparent.

'Your father . . .'

'If we're going to start with my father, you can leave right away . . .'

'Your mother . . .'

'Likewise.'

'Your sister.'

'What's happening with my sister?'

Every fortress has a weak point that can be breached. Carvalho told the story of the police round-up, and this thoroughly modern youth, a positive caricature of a yuppie, didn't turn a hair. He allowed him to say his piece, and his face revealed a state of increasing dissatisfaction.

'You're not telling me anything I didn't know already. I knew about her arrest, because I was the one who pulled the strings to get her out in the first place.'

'Your father says it was him.'

'All he did was dot the "I"s. It was me who set up all the connections. A publishing house like ours has a lot of connections. There's nobody of any importance who doesn't aspire to publishing his memoirs with us one of these days, because we pay best, and we sell most. I've just signed a contract for an *Autobiography of Franco*.'

'*The* Franco?'

'No. A communist writer, very communist: I laid my cheque on the table — I'm not going to tell you how much — and all his prejudices disappeared in an instant. He asked for guarantees of editorial freedom, and I promised as much as he wanted; that gives me time to work on him when he comes round for the second cheque.'

'Is there always a second cheque?'

'That's the best system. One cheque to buy, and the other to kill! I'm sorry that you don't seem to have anything to sell me.'

Carvalho was silent for a moment, and looked him in the eye:

'People don't always sell what they have; sometimes they sell what they don't have.'

Brando Junior turned this proposition over in his mind and gave Carvalho an interested look.

'I have my professional deontology, señor Brando. You can ask anyone in the trade, including the police, and people who can't stand the sight of me, and they'll tell you that I am loyal to my clients to the end, even if I think a particular client's an arsehole. In that case everything finishes when I hand over my report, and I let it be understood that I think he's an arsehole. But I never abandon a case. My job is to unravel the mystery, and after that it's not up to me to worry what the warehousemen of mysteries are going to do with the mystery, let alone the gelders of mysteries, the vampires of mysteries ... clients, police, judges ... that's not my job. There was a time when I studied philosophy, and they taught me what it was all about: they taught me that it involved stripping away veils from the goddess, and behind the last veil you find the truth. I believe the technique is known as *alezeia*, or maybe it isn't a technique but one way among others of allowing yourself to believe that there are still veils to be stripped.'

Brando was bored with all this philosophy, even if it was Greek, but he pretended to be interested. Obviously well brought-up. But in the end he said in an icy tone:

'I can do without the theory of the novel. Could you get to the point, please.'

'You pulled the strings to get your sister out. It stands to reason that you also knew why she was there, or at least you know what the police know, and it would be worth your while to know if they have let you in on what the political bosses of the police know. All this is going to involve me in days and days of work, sniffing around, turning over the shit, aspects of the question which your father isn't concerned about, because he enjoys telling it like it is ... By the way, are you also the kind of person who enjoys telling it like it is?'

'I detest people who take a special pride in being outspoken.'

The boy wasn't as misbegotten as he seemed, but he probably could be if he so decided. He puffed himself up in his directorial swivel chair, put the fingertips of both hands together and raised them to his lips, as if he was working out which of Carvalho's orifices he should put the lethal bullet through.

'If I allow you to see some notes, which are the outcome of my good offices with the authorities, can you assure me that you will treat this case as closed? I am prepared to add a cheque of my own to what my father is going to pay.'

'Your father's will do to buy, and yours will do to kill.'

'I took over a business that was at death's door, and set it straight in five days flat. When my father inherited it, it was a going concern, but he took it down some pretty weird paths just to satisfy his ego. I am very concerned that my sister's escapades don't reflect back on the publishing house, because at this moment we are negotiating an input of foreign capital which is going to triple our value. As you see, I'm showing you my cards; however, I won't have you thinking that this means you can play with them.'

'All I can promise you is that if you tell me that a job's already been done, then I won't have to do it.'

'I'm going to take that as a promise, and now I'm going to ask you to do something else for me — you will naturally be reimbursed. Follow my sister, and see what you can do to stop her getting into more of the same kind of trouble.'

'First I'd like to read those notes.'

Brando Junior went across the room, walking as if his suit was made of silk. As indeed it was. He walked well, and his movements were those of a young athlete before he's sprained a joint or torn a ligament. You only understand what it is to walk well when you've seen a young athlete before he's gone and broken something. A small quantity of this graceful walking took him to a set of shelves which were made of the wood from a forest even older than that which had supplied the raw material for his father's desk, and from a desk whose key was visible but at the same time invisible he took a letter-file made of a leather so fine that it was like human skin. He put it on the desk, within Carvalho's reach. As the detective leaned over to open it, the yuppie proclaimed: 'This isn't a reading room.'

'Beatriz Brando Matasanz, also known as "Beba", a minor, was observed on three occasions in the streets immediately surrounding the Arco del Teatro, where she was asking around for drugs, preferably cocaine, in quantities suitable for personal use. As a result we limited ourselves to a routine observation, to identify her connections within the network of small dealers. Her most regular dealer is Belisario Bird, alias Palomo, Honduran by nationality, connected to the Perla clan, who normally operates in the rectangle between calle Barbera, San Olegario, Arco del Teatro and the Ramblas. When Palomo was interrogated at the request of the subscriber to this report, he confirmed earlier reports as to the frequency of sales to the above-mentioned, although he made clear that he could not answer for other purchases that she may have made around Plaza Real, where she has also been observed acting in a suspicious manner, although less frequently than in the area referred to above. During the short period she was in detention, she was not pressured in the usual manner, for obvious reasons; however she stated that she had never bought drugs of any kind, and that she had only ever smoked one "joint" (slang term for marijuana cigarette), a long time ago, and it had made her feel sick. When it was suggested that it was strange for a young girl of her age to be around those parts, she stated that she had a vocation as a writer, ever since she had won a prize in a regional poetry competition, and she needed to see how different classes of people lived in the city. When she was warned about the dangers of this way of carrying on, she used the example of the police themselves, who risked their lives in dangerous places for motives that were professional, just like her own. In a more relaxed conversation with Inspector Vinuesa Cobos, the woman officer in charge of the minor offenders section, she re-stated her need to explore all aspects of the city, and said that she was thinking of joining the police anti-narcotics section, to get a closer view of how they operate. Inspector Vinuesa Cobos then wrote a favourable report on her case, although with some observations on the need for someone with moral authority over señorita Brando Matasanz to keep an eye on her activities, and to be aware that her idealism was likely to end her up in some rather unpleasant situations which she was too young to deal with yet. The writer of this present report would not have given her so much benefit of the doubt, because at several points during her interrogation he suspected that she was very good at putting up red herrings. She seemed to have few scruples about distinguishing truth from falsehood, a condition which the writer has often noticed among young people, inasmuch as young people today are a lot more prepared to lie than in previous times, a fact which, while not immediately relevant to the case, could be due to the quantity of falsehoods which our young people absorb from their earliest infancy through television and decadent songs. These fill their heads with amoral images which sooner or later are bound to show up in an amoral approach to their own lives. For this reason, and also because the writer of this report feels a shared responsibility, in his capacity as an officer of the law and as a father, I would suggest that the Inspector's advice should be acted on, but that somebody should also intervene with a heavy hand, assuming that there is someone in a position to do so, to preserve the healthy parts, which otherwise might soon end up rotten too.'

Police prose had improved a lot since Carvalho last had occasion to read police reports; and the language of the report compared favourably with his frequent run-ins with Contreras and other officers of the law, whose chosen mode of discourse was still much the same as it had always been, aggressive and full of threatening silences. For the umpteenth time he reflected on the hypocrisy of culture. For the writer of the report it had been easy to pick up a pen, and go into the communicative mode; but face to face, *viva voce*, his syntax would not have been quite so florid and rhetorical; the clauses and sub-clauses would have given way to grunts, heavy breathing, expletives and muttered curses. At no point did the report say how much of this information came from Belisario Bird, confidant and small-time dealer. Ever since the death of Bromide, Carvalho had been in the dark as he moved through the city's underworld. All the rats nowadays belonged to a new generation, and Carvalho refused to allow himself to go and look for new informants. It was as if not looking for a replacement for Bromide was an act of posthumous fidelity — fidelity not only to the shoe-shine, but also to himself, and to a city which was already dying in his memory and which no longer existed in his desires. What was happening was the death of a city in which compassion was a human necessity, and the birth of a city in which the only thing that mattered was the distance between buying your-self and selling yourself.

He was incapable of admitting that his body was getting old, let alone worrying about it. But he was terrified at the thought of his memory ageing, as if the progressive distancing of the present and of the future was going to represent a death sentence on a series of people and situations who had trusted in him to make them immortal. And in the metamorphosis of his Barcelona there was something at work — an implac-able exercise in sadism — which was going to destroy even the cemeteries of his memory, the physical space where the protagonists of his memories might have been able to live on. The fact that he missed Bromide, the shoe-shine who had acted as his informant in exchange for a few pesetas and a sympathetic ear for his descriptions of his days as a young legionnaire in the service of General Franco, was also related to his concern for the survival of the physical space in which he used to meet the old man — the bars, the street corners, and the miserable boarding-house, which was now threatened by the demolition of part of the Barrio Chino. On occasion he would bump into *El Mohammed*, who, according to what Bromide had told him, was the best informed man in the Barrio Chino: 'There's not a knifing in this city that he doesn't know about.' At the start, *el morito*, as Bromide called him, used to smile at him from a distance, with the complicity of a man who had once come to blows with him, as if to assure him that one of these days he was going to get his own back.

But one day he came over to him with his tense smile of a barbarian from the South.

'You need me, Stupid. You should know that. The hunter's best friend is the ferret. If a clever person doesn't know what he needs, then he's not a clever person, he's just stupid.'

There he went again, with his absurd logical propositions which almost always wound up with the word 'stupid'. Carvalho had given as good as he'd got on the occasion of his fight with the Arab. This was during his investigation of the case of the death threats against the centre-forward, at about the time he'd been present at Bromide's death bed. But now every time *El Mohammed* offered his services, the ex-legionnaire shoe-shine must have been spinning in the plot that Carvalho and Charo had rented for him in the Montjuich cemetery.

'I'm getting less and less work these days. I feel like retiring.'

The Arab looked him up and down, and shook his head as if not liking what he saw.

'If as well as being stupid you feel you're getting old, the best thing that can happen to you is for the desert sands to swallow you up.'

'I'll try it at the first opportunity.'

But without even realizing it, he found himself walking in streets where he knew he might meet *El Mohammed* — whose real name he didn't know — and he felt cheated when he didn't run into him. Was it sensible to be so faithful to Bromide as to deny himself the services of a reliable informant? The city's underworld still had its own codes of practice, and what was happening there bore no resemblance to what was happening on the surface. Fifty years previously it had been the Murcian and Andalucian immigrants who had built their slums along these streets; now it was the North Africans. Fifty years ago, the underworld was controlled by marginalized individuals — or self-marginalized, like Bromide — in exchange for a relativized poverty, and now this position was passing on to the barbarians from the South who had penetrated Europe from the bottom, in the same way that the Germans had penetrated it from the top. The Germans had initially tried to overcome the Roman Empire by force of arms, and since this had proved impossible they had infiltrated it instead, and had ended up as the policemen of that Empire. By then it was theirs. Right now, the barbarians from the South were in the process of taking over the leftovers, and Carvalho couldn't help seeing in them an instrument of justice against the country's revolting self-complacency.

'Have Contreras's boys been back in touch?'

'No.'

'Charo?'

'No.'

'Brando?'

'No.'

'And . . .?'

'No.'

He contained his desire to go looking for Lebrun and Claire, because he wanted to avoid putting Contreras and Co. onto the trail of his desire, or didn't want to shatter the few desires left to him. Once they had completed their journey through the labyrinth, Claire with her Greek, and Lebrun with his, they had fulfilled the purpose of their voyage, and each of them had left, leaving Carvalho behind to continue in his role as an accompanist to other searchers after indispensible truths. The sooner he sorted himself out the better. His body was all in one piece, Biscuter had already paid in Lebrun's cheque, and Brando Senior's bill was going to be peanuts compared with what he was going to charge Brando Junior. And when all was said and done, setting himself on the trail of señorita Brando meant going up a peg or two, because he was no longer just a sniffer of pricks, but a sniffer of cunt, and who knows, perhaps one day that naked angel would devote herself to sniffing round the more intimate parts of his own body. Why would señorita Brando be after drugs? This sounded like the title of a low-budget TV film, but it was the question he had to address. He had to do something to justify his bill. He parked out in front of a villa which had the air of belonging to a man who was insufficiently rich or a man who was insufficient because he was rich. Brando Senior had warned him that Beba generally got up late and in a bad mood, which meant that she would usually stay at home, in her room, with the curtains drawn, listening to records, with the volume high enough to blow her speakers and blast out the neighbouring villas, despite the gardens in between. Then, as evening fell, Beba would eat whatever was in the fridge, would dress as scantily as the season permitted, and would emerge onto the street, from where she would sometimes return straight away, but more often in the early hours of the morning, by which time her father would have got bored with waiting up to meet whoever her new boyfriend was, rather than having the surprise the next morning when he would find them in his office feasting on toast and Nutella, the girl's favourite dish. It was ten o'clock at night, and Carvalho was already promising himself that next time he would ask to be informed in advance of the schedule that his prey customarily kept, when finally the front door opened and Beba leapt out to meet the street as if she had been imprisoned indoors all day. Carvalho lit the Rey del Mundo which he had just taken the band off, but he had to light it fast to keep up with the fast-moving VW. Beba headed for the area of Gracia, and blithely parked in a no-parking zone. She looked good, walking on air like a small-scale goddess. Carvalho tried to erase the word 'goddess' from his mental vocabulary, because it felt like an old man's word, a recognition that there was a distance, necessarily irremediable, between him and her. At the bar, she exchanged greetings with various

people, and went over to the counter, where a young
man was waiting for her. He kissed her in a manner that
suggested they were acting the closing sequence of a
romantic movie. Carvalho didn't know what to do with
himself. There were others of his age there, but they
were dressed to look twenty years younger, whereas on
that particular night he himself was biologically at his
most sincere, since it was two days since he'd last had a
shave. He propped himself on the bar next to Beba and
met the bartender's worried look. He thought he
should probably order something aggressive in order
to cancel out the impression that he was a police
officer, so he asked for a straight malt whisky, a double,
the best in the house. This only served to increase the
barman's suspicions, but Carvalho could live with that,
and when he had drunk the whisky in two or three sips
he began studying the place, and its inhabitants, with all
the disdain that is deserved by things and people that
don't accept us. For instance, the idiot with a green
crest of hair on his head, who, as Carvalho went to light
his half-smoked Rey del Mundo, was already waving
his hand around to object to the smoke, in a place that
already reeked of marijuana and brilliantine. At two in
the morning, Beba suddenly gave her companion a
hefty slap. The slap was not returned. The young man
spat right by her feet, and abandoned her in the middle
of the dance floor, where Beba continued dancing,
studiously ignoring his departure. When the number
was over, Beba wandered around the club, sidestepping
couples and peering at shadows, while Carvalho asked
for his bill and left a 1,000-peseta tip for the barman,

who was relieved because who's ever heard of a cop leaving a 1,000-peseta tip?

'Some guava tree, eh?'

For all that the grateful barman tried to see a guava tree, he couldn't. When Carvalho pointed to Beba, who was still searching around, the penny dropped.

'The chick there? Very nice. But completely crazy... She thinks she's... I don't know... she thinks she's...'

He didn't know, and he fell silent, and returned to his job, in the secretly programmed manner of all the best barmen. Beba had her arms round another girl and was deep in passionate conversation which she suddenly broke off, then returned to the bar. Carvalho moved like a footballer getting ready to receive a ball which is about to fall just right. Beba landed a couple of yards away, and ordered herself a non-alcoholic beer. Carvalho was well placed to strike up conversation.

'On the hard stuff, I see.'

Beba looked at him, and seemed not to like what she saw. Unlikely that she had recognized him from the opening of her bedroom door. It was simply that Carvalho wasn't her type. As the detective was searching to extend his opening gambit, she got in first.

'What would you like to drink?'

'Whisky. When I'm in the mood for doing nothing and don't know what to do anyway, I drink whisky.'

'And when you have things to do?'

'Wine.'

Beba gave a small grimace of distaste that seemed more directed at herself than at Carvalho.

'I see you know how to look after yourself. That was quite a slap you gave your friend.'

'I can't stand self-centred people.'

'Is your friend self-centred?'

'That's all he is. He should have it stamped on his I.D. card — "profession: Egotist". I asked him to take me up to see the "lollipop" — that amazing aerial they're building on the side of Tibidabo. He said he didn't want to.'

'Did he indeed?!'

'Yes he did.'

'How very soul-less of him.'

She liked this word. She nodded, and had tears in her eyes.

'Soul-less, that's exactly what he is. He's got no soul.'

'If you're really so upset about not driving up there, I could take you. It's very near my house. I live in Vallvidrera.'

Beba placed her hand on her chest and shut her eyes.

'You don't owe me anything, but that pig owes me a lot of favours.'

She had a primitive but effective morality. Exchange and barter. It was all too easy to guess what she had given the egotist, so easy in fact that Carvalho thought that maybe he was mistaken.

'To see him walking round, you'd think he was a real tough guy. But he seems to have decided he's gay. Am I boring you?'

No, she wasn't boring him at all. If she was drunk, it would have been on non-alcoholic beer; in fact she had probably been drunk all day without any need for alcohol. The story began with a body-building contest which the egotist had entered, and an attempt to strike up a relationship with her, which had come to nothing because he couldn't deliver the goods. Apparently he had a complex about being underdeveloped, and in the muscle-show parades he used to tuck a falsie down his crutch, so that man's favourite muscle — and that of a few women too — wouldn't end up looking ridiculous in comparison with his biceps and triceps ... She had asked him to show it to her.

'"Show it to me, Juan Carlos, I insist ..." I said. And he started crying — imagine it, a grown man, crying like a kid. Then he showed it to me, and I began to smile.'

She smiled again. She smiled like an angel, a thoroughly feminine angel. And when she smiled, it was as if the disco music for street-wise adolescents had suddenly given way to a Hungarian violin playing romantic interludes for late-afternoon melodramas.

'No. It isn't small at all, Juan Carlos. It's perfectly normal. Anyway, what matters isn't the size, but the quality of your desire, and your ability to love your partner.'

She said it with the voice of a sixteen-year-old. If she had said it with the voice of a thirty-year-old, a forty-year old, or a fifty-year-old, Carvalho would already have been looking for a corner of the club where he could either laugh or throw up, but that voice of crystal could have said absolutely anything and still transmit sincerity. She had read a novel, once, all about the Spanish civil war, yes, that was it, the Spanish civil war, the one that happened all those years ago, when the Russians had seized her grandfather's publishing house, yes, of course it was Russians, because they were all over the place in those days. The novel told the story of a nurse and a prisoner of war, or perhaps he wasn't a prisoner of war, but somebody who'd been wounded in the war, because whenever you come across a nurse in a war novel, there's bound to be a wounded hero too. And the soldier was so sad and so badly wounded that the nurse had made love with him, as an act of generosity.

'Or of the communion of saints,' Carvalho interjected, temporarily throwing her.

'Communion of what?'

'The communion of saints, the forgiveness of sins, the resurrection of the body . . . the Final Judgement.'

'Are you religious?'

'They tried to get me into Catholicism once, but I got out fast as soon as I realized that most of the things that I enjoyed weren't allowed.'

'I can't stand religious people. We've had a very deep conversation, haven't we? The trouble is, everywhere's full of vultures these days. My brother, for instance. My brother is a one hundred per cent stainless steel vulture!'

The angel had a wonderful way with adjectives.

'Are your parents the same way?'

'I haven't yet decided what kind of animal my father is. All I know is, he's an idiot.'

'And your mother . . .? Is she around . . .?'

'My mother is an athlete.'

Obviously, filial love was laying it on a bit, but

Carvalho accepted her judgement with a complicity that was almost enthusiastic.

'Do you mean she practises athletics?'

'Spiritual athletics.'

She dug around in her handbag and pulled out a book. *Peter Pan.* She flicked through it, as if she knew what she was looking for. As she thumbed her way obsessively through the pages, she told him about the best definition of a mother that she had ever come across. 'Tinkerbell,' she said. 'A real mother has to be like Tinkerbell.' Finally she found the paragraph she was looking for, and with a radiant look in her eyes she handed it to Carvalho.

'There, read on from there . . .'

Carvalho looked to right and left. Fortunately nobody seemed to have noticed what was going on, though the barman still had a firm eye on them, and this particular eye was sending a message of malicious complicity in his direction. Hadn't he told him that she was completely crazy? And so it was that Carvalho set about reading *Peter Pan*, at the precise moment where Captain Hook proposes to Wendy that she becomes the mother of all of them, so moved is he by the example of Tinkerbell. Carvalho nodded, as if he was totally convinced, but he suddenly realized that he was emotionally tired, and offered to see her home.

'To my home?'

He could just imagine the look on the face of Brando Senior when he came down to breakfast the following day, to find Carvalho and his daughter feasting together on toast and Nutella.

'No. I'll just see you to your car. Something to get my muscles moving . . .'

She didn't say no. She went out ahead of him, and the barman seized the opportunity to lean over the bar and ask:

'*Peter Pan*? She showed you a book called *Peter Pan*, didn't she?'

Carvalho wasted precious moments justifying himself, and then justifying her, and by the time he got out into the street, the VW was roaring down the street, with Wendy on board.

Inspector Contreras requested his presence at police headquarters. A dead man had turned up, and the inspector had been informed that Carvalho had been looking for the man in question some days previously.

And he had been informed correctly.

Every time that Inspector Contreras wanted to remind a private detective that he was just a piece of shit, he usually picked on Carvalho. This was possibly because he saw him as the most insubordinate of this lower species of humanity and as such capable of giving as much contempt as he got. As for Carvalho, he saw Contreras simply as a policeman, a specialist in repression in the pay of whoever most benefited from that repression. He recognized that this was a theoretical principle inherited from his anarchist youth, from his pre- or post-Marxist adolescence, and that it was utopian — and dangerous too — to dream of a world without police. But we all have the right to hang onto at least part of our own rhetoric, and, what's more, his relations with Contreras had enabled him to add specific justifications to this basic principle. Today's encounter was no exception. Carvalho had to wait for an hour and a half, stuck in a corridor, kicking his heels. Every now and then he found himself on the receiving end of menacing looks from one of Contreras's subordinates, and several times a dismissive snort, which was a frank declaration of none-too-friendly corporate relations. In the end he was ushered into the office of the inspector, who raised his head just sufficiently to give him a look of weary contempt. The inspector appeared to be very busy with his paperwork, and only left off his concentration when Carvalho sat down without asking permission. Carvalho smiled amiably while he waited for the angry tirade that he could feel brewing. In an attempt to postpone its arrival, he proceeded to make a visual inventory of everything in the office, and all of a sudden there was his torch, pleading with him to recognize its presence. 'Here I am, it's me, don't you recognize me?' There it was, with its fluted cylinder, onto which some drops of black paint had fallen at some indeterminate time in the past. He made a determined effort to ignore it.

'How did you come to know Alekos Farandouris?'

But the torch was insistently still there, and he could almost feel its volume, and the fluting on its body, and the warmth of its light in his hand, as if he were still shining it down the labyrinth which led to Alekos Farandouris. Contreras repeated his question, and from the tone of his voice it was obvious that he had sufficient information for Carvalho not to bother to play dumb, feigning surprise at the name of Alekos. And what would happen if he tried to get his torch back? Presumably they'd never trace it back to him ...

or maybe if he admitted having investigated the case, he'd be able to reclaim it officially — that's my torch. But it would take several months before he ever got it back — if the judge decided that it was circumstantial evidence — and what the torch was asking was to be rescued straight away. What person, or object, would want to stay in a police station a moment longer than necessary? Not even a policeman! Contreras was now frowning. He got up. He walked round for a bit, all the while glaring at Carvalho. Finally he stopped, turned towards him, and took a deep breath. The torch offered Carvalho a word of advice: 'Don't let yourself be intimidated by what he's saying. And get me out of here, please, get me out of here.'

'How do you come to know Alekos Farandouris, señor Carvalho?'

The 'señor Carvalho' indicated that Contreras was making an initial effort at restraint, an effort which Carvalho appreciated, for which reason he pretended to abandon all mental resistance, and replied in a relaxed tone:

'I never actually got to know him.'

Contreras sighed, and seemed to find a refutation on a highly important piece of paper which he proceeded to wave under Carvalho's nose.

'I see that we're getting off on the wrong foot here. Here it says that you were chasing all over Barcelona looking for Alekos Farandouris, as if it was a matter of life or death. You weren't on your own, but as soon as they told me the description of the group, I thought to myself: "Aha! That's Carvalho!" And then it turns out that a few hours after señor Carvalho went looking for him, Alekos Farandouris turns up dead of a drug overdose, an overdose big enough to kill a horse, and now I, as you with your native quickwittedness will understand, find myself obliged to ask: "Why were you in such a hurry to chase after that particular corpse?"'

Carvalho cleared his throat and drew drops of the most innocent innocence into his eyes.

'All I can tell you is that when I left señor Farandouris in the early hours of Thursday morning, he was in fine form — at death's door, I would say.'

'That doesn't tell me why you were so interested in tracking down this corpse.'

'To cut a long story short, Inspector Contreras, I shall give credit to your intelligence. What interest do you think I had in finding a dying Greek?'

'You're a mercenary, of course, and that's what I'm referring to. Who was paying you to look for this Greek?'

'His relations. They contacted me from France. They were worried because he had disappeared, and they asked me to find him. They knew that he was somewhere in Barcelona, and they chose me because I now have an international reputation.'

'Congratulations.'

'Logically speaking, if you're looking for an artist, you go and look among artists. I can tell you that finding him was relatively easy, even though I shall be telling my clients that it was extremely difficult, in order to justify my fee.'

'I understand, I understand.'

'And that's all there is to it. I last saw Farandouris in an abandoned warehouse in Pueblo Nuevo, where I'd gone to find him thanks to information from people who knew him. He was very ill. I would say he didn't have long to live, although he didn't know it, or perhaps he just wasn't wanting to admit it.'

'And you just left him there?'

'He wasn't willing to move.'

'Did you go there on your own?'

'No.'

'Would you care to tell me who you went with, then?'

'No. I don't think it would add anything to what you already know, or what you need to know. That information comes under the heading of professional confidentiality. I stand by what I said, though: if Farandouris wasn't dead when I saw him, it could only have been a matter of time. He looked extremely ill.'

'He was.'

'AIDS?'

'Well spotted. You have a diagnostic eye.'

'He looked the sort to have some fashionable disease.'

'Since he arrived in Barcelona eight months ago, Carvalho, he was hospitalized on three occasions, and the last time he just walked out without so much as a goodbye. He was past curing, and simply disappeared. Now he reappears, dead. And not, in fact, in an old warehouse, señor Carvalho, but on a beach.'

'Did he have the hypodermic with him?'

Contreras didn't reply immediately. He was probably analysing the reason for the question, or how much interest Carvalho had in knowing the answer. Not very much, as it turned out. As far as Contreras could see, he appeared more interested in the objects piled on his desk.

'He did.'

'Good. Case closed! It wouldn't be the first case of a foreign vagrant giving himself an overdose as a way of putting an end to it all.'

'No. He wouldn't be the first. But there were a lot of people out looking for him, and, more to the point, you're the only person who can lead us to his relations, in the event that they might want to retrieve his body to give it a decent Christian burial.'

'I shall try to contact my clients.'

'We found his passport. It gives an address in Paris — a hotel, not a private house. A relatively recent passport. He only stayed in that hotel for the time necessary to get his passport through. Curious, really — as if he was trying to erase his tracks.'

'Does he have a police record?'

'No, he's clean. If he'd had a record, we'd have sorted him out by now.'

'Would you mind if I see his passport? I'd like to see the photo. To make sure we're talking about the same man.'

Contreras shrugged, and tossed the passport over. Carvalho got up and leaned against the desk, which was covered with sheets of paper, files and various bits and pieces, including his torch. He picked up the passport, opened it at the page with the photograph, and raised it to his eyes as if he was having problems seeing it properly. Contreras appeared to have his mind on something else during the time that Carvalho was engaged in this operation. The detective then leaned abruptly across the desk to hold the passport under the light of the desk lamp. His brusque action meant that his left elbow swept some of the papers and files to the floor, along with his torch.

'Oh hell, I'm sorry, Inspector.'

Contreras belonged to that race of people that includes husbands who get irritable when their wives break a glass in the sink, and fathers who shout at their children when they accidentally spill their milk. Clumsy people annoyed him, and he glared at Carvalho accusingly, while at the same time indicating that he should immediately remedy the situation.

'That's all I need — you adding to the mess in this office.'

Apologizing profusely, Carvalho ducked down behind the desk, picked up the torch and put it in his jacket pocket. Then he continued slowly picking up the files and papers and placed them back on the desk so that Contreras could check them one by one, frowning all the while.

'Is that the lot?'

'Yes,' Carvalho lied, from where he was down on his knees. At the same time he kept one hand on the torch in his pocket just in case Contreras noticed it was missing. However the inspector seemed satisfied to have his papers back, and was more or less ignoring Carvalho, who was now back on his feet in front of him.

'I'm grateful that you've been so understanding,

Inspector, but urgent business calls, and I'm afraid I can't stay in your charming company for much longer.'

'I want the details of his relations, these clients of yours.'

'I'm sure you'll understand, I have to speak with them first. I can't pass on the information just like that. But I can promise you'll be hearing from me soon.'

'I'll be hearing from you a lot sooner than you think, if you start fucking around with me.'

At last the animal in him had come out. There was nothing to indicate that he was intending to stop him leaving, but as from this moment Carvalho knew that he was going to have Contreras breathing down his neck. For this reason, when he emerged onto the street he took no particular direction, and strolled down by the Moll de la Fusta, with one hand on his grateful torch and his eyes on Mariscal's giant prawn. He found a phone booth and rang the Palace Hotel. Neither Monsieur Lebrun nor Mademoiselle Claire were at the hotel. They had checked out the previous day, and had left for an unknown destination. They'd certainly managed to make time and space for themselves, but there was still Carvalho, and they had counted too much on his respect for professional confidentiality. Or maybe his feeling of unease had been built into their game plan. As for Carvalho, he was simply suffering on account of Claire, and hoping that he'd be able to get to her before Contreras did.

He resumed his perambulations, allowing time to fill the distance between one phone box and the next, and this time his call took him to the Olympic Office, to

Colonel Parra. He was in a meeting, very much in a meeting, his secretary insisted, and, in the face of Carvalho's insistence, she added that he was having a discussion with the mayor.

'The mayor still has at least another twelve months in office, miss. Whereas what I have here is a matter of life and death.'

In the end a ruffled and justifiably irritated ex-Colonel Parra came onto the line.

'I need to know whether the Frenchman I was asking about, the one from French television, is still in Barcelona, or whether he's finished and gone.'

'Is that all?'

'It's more than enough, I promise you.'

'Can you justify pulling me out of a meeting with no less a person than the mayor himself, just for this?'

'You've known Pascual for half a lifetime.'

'That's not funny.'

'This is a matter of life and death, Colonel. It's serious.'

Parra cleared his throat, mollified by Carvalho's use of this informal title which brought back some of his best memories. He sent the required information down the line.

'As it turns out, Georges Lebrun must still be in Barcelona, because he rang to arrange a meeting with me tomorrow morning.'

'Did he leave an address or a phone number?'

'No. The appointment is for half past ten. That's all I can tell you.'

And he hung up. That's what friends are for, thought

Carvalho. In the old days there wouldn't have been enough hours in the day for their conversations on the accumulation of capital, or the transition from quantity to quality within the theoretical constructs of dialectical materialism. And Franco. And Lumumba. And Uncle Tom Cobley and all. Now Parra was annoyed because Carvalho had turned up as a glitch in his conversation with the mayor. But the detective had more pressing things on his mind — in order to reach Claire all he had was this piece of information about Lebrun and the fact of an appointment the following morning. That would be too late. Biscuter was waiting for him with a meal prepared: fried fish, aubergines, peppers and *pan con tomate*. This was what Carvalho called his 'señora Paca' treat, in honour of his grandmother, and the meal was accompanied by a suggestion from Biscuter.

'I've got a brilliant recipe here, boss — Majorca vegetable casserole and beef done with *salsa verde*. Very low-calorie. Very good for you.'

'Where would you look, to find a foreign male accompanied by a beautiful Greek teenager, and possibly also a woman who is distraught, or who's pretending she's distraught?'

'The questions you ask, boss! Are the foreign man and the teenager having an affair?'

'I don't know. It's pretty weird.'

'Check out the clubs. You'll have a lot of time to kill first. People like that only come out like snails at night. And what are you going to do about señor Brando? He never stops ringing.'

What *was* he going to do with señor Brando, the

ex-señora Brando, the ex-athlete, the son, the daughter, the whole bunch of them...? He invented an excuse for Biscuter to pass on, but realized that in fact it was directed to himself.

'I don't see how I can carry on with the case, Biscuter. I've made every mistake in the book.'

'You've been having a rough time, eh, boss?'

'And it looks like it's not going to get any better. How would you fancy dropping your apron for a couple of days and getting on the trail?'

With Beba he now found himself in the worst of strategic positions. If he followed her openly, she would recognize him, and if he actually approached her it would probably result in a relationship which would come under the heading not of the corruption of minors, but the corruption of adults. He thought of cooling off for a couple of days, but the trouble was that the teenage goddess had wings and could end up just about anywhere, from north to south, from land to water, from air to fire, as if everything attracted her and bored her at the same time. Biscuter was excited to discover that Carvalho needed him for something more than cooking, answering the phone and complaining because he hadn't carried out his promise to send his assistant to Paris on a haute cuisine course the first part of which was only soups.

'Follow her, Biscuter. But be careful if she heads for the Barrio Chino. Understand? Because if there's a police round-up you'll be in big trouble.'

'Is something wrong again, boss?'

'All I'm trying to say is that if the cops find you there,

they'll run you in straight away. You have the kind of face that says you don't have a lawyer.'

'You must have had a hell of a day, boss. I'll put my Sunday suit on.'

Even worse, thought Carvalho, as he imagined the sight of this half-pint in a Sunday suit, but he didn't say anything so as not to offend him. Having placed the Brando family under Biscuter's protection, Carvalho could now return to his obsession with Claire.

'Boss, you're going to have to give me some money for expenses. When you follow somebody, you have to hand out tips left right and centre, and buy things so as to cover your tracks. Sometimes you have to go into bookshops and buy books or magazines. I won't be able to do that out of the money that you give me for shopping and office expenses.'

'Watch out what you buy, Biscuter.'

He invaded Biscuter's private cubicle to give him five thousand pesetas for expenses and found him in the act of putting deodorant under his skinny armpits. Biscuter withdrew the deodorant hastily, annoyed at Carvalho's invasion of his privacy. He'd also put brilliantine on his red hair, transforming his head into a scene from some ecological disaster. Biscuter's shoulder blades looked as if they were detached from his body, like two little bony wings contained within a sleeveless vest that was old but clean. Biscuter had the shoulders of a tuber-culosis victim of the 1940s, or of somebody suffering from pleurisy. Did people still get pleurisy these days, Carvalho wondered.

'Best wrap up warm.'

He left Biscuter looking puzzled, because that autumn was especially warm, and he emerged onto the street mentally castigating whoever it was who had once said that the best plan was to have no plan. He walked round the Barrio Chino a couple of times and ducked down every alley he came to in case any of Contreras's boys were following him. He couldn't afford to waste time, though, so he took a cab to the Palace Hotel, telling the driver to change direction several times. Finally, when he got to the hotel, the receptionist confirmed what he had told him on the phone.

'Did they leave together?'

'Together, and with all their luggage. It must have been a last-minute decision, because they originally booked their rooms for a fortnight.'

'Did they leave in the same cab? Where did they ask to be taken?'

'You'd best have a word with the doorman.'

They had left in the same taxi, and they had looked as if they were going to the airport. Even though they hadn't said as much.

'I can always tell when people are going to the airport. I don't know how or why. Must be the way they look at us when they leave, or the way they sit in the cab.'

'Was the taxi driver one of the hotel's regulars?'

'We don't have regular cabbies. But I know the man. His name's Lorenzo. You'll find him either driving round here, or on the taxi rank where Gran Via crosses Catalunya. Sometimes his nephew drives the cab because he's out doing a newspaper run.'

'Which paper?'

'*Avui,* I think. The Catalan daily.'

An invisible clock in his head told him that it was time to eat, but by this time he had reached the conclusion that today was Lorenzo's taxi day, not his newspaper day. It had been his nephew who had been on shift that morning, and nobody knew, or wanted to say, where he lived. He did at least discover where the van was parked, in a small warehouse in calle Parlamento, but vans don't talk, and there was no sign of a tax disc with the man's details in the van's windows. He had no time to return to the office to try Biscuter's menu, so instead he had a bite to eat in the area, and proved to himself yet again the depressing fact that *tapas* were not what they used to be — or maybe he was just getting more demanding. An after-dinner drowsiness found him standing, disoriented, in the middle of the pavement on Paralelo. Maybe if he were to let himself be swept along by his adolescent impulse and head for where the Ramblas runs down to the port, he might meet the woman he had always dreamt of, the woman that he had been waiting for ever since he first started dreaming about women. In the end, he decided against wallowing in sentiment and set off for the Palace Hotel, like a man returning to the source of his confusion, in the hope of turning up fresh clues there.

'Lorenzo has just dropped by,' the doorman announced, watching as Carvalho's hand reached for his wallet and his fingers hesitated between a five-hundred note and a thousand note.

'I told him what you were trying to find out, and he told me something.'

Carvalho's fingers settled on the thousand-peseta note.

'He took them to the airport.'

'Both of them?'

'Both of them. First thing on Thursday morning, first flight out. They looked very tired, and she was very off-colour, very depressed, apparently.'

'Are you sure he left them at the airport?'

'Sure.'

But Lebrun had not left. Why not? And what had he done with Mitia? What's more, he had made an appointment to see Colonel Parra in the Olympic office at ten-thirty the following morning. Or maybe this had just been a cover to enable Claire to escape. And what about Dimitrios? Carvalho reckoned that the police wouldn't be pursuing the case too hard. From their point of view the best foreign drug addict was a dead one, but he was going to have to give Contreras a sensible answer as to where Alekos's body was to be sent. He remembered again how Georges and Claire had reacted to the two men at the moment of discovering them.

'Alekos,' she had said.

'Mitia,' he had said.

And there was no sign of Mitia in their group, unless he had been waiting to meet them at the airport. He restrained his initial impulse to rush straight to the airport to check the passenger lists for the flights to Paris that Thursday morning. It wouldn't take

Contreras long to find out that he'd been there. When
the travel agencies opened in the afternoon, all it took
was a visit to Air France for him to experience a
complex mixture of relief and anxiety. A Claire Delmas
had travelled to Paris on the first flight on Thursday
morning. But not Lebrun. Nor was there anyone who
sounded like Mitia. Unless they had left Spain by
another route, Lebrun and Mitia were still in Barcelona,
and had succeeded in getting the woman onto the other
side of the safety line. He would need to curb his
impatience and let the hours pass. He would need to
wait till the evening before he could begin his search for
Lebrun. His plan was to engineer a seemingly casual
encounter, to get to Lebrun before his planned appointment in the morning, and before Contreras's
inevitable phone call with new facts which would place
Claire dangerously in the foreground. With luck this
encounter would finally clarify what had happened
that night in the warehouse.

Lebrun was not the sort of man to go slumming, but
he did enjoy visual excitement, fresh visual blood for
his eyes to feast on. As the daylight began to fail and
night prepared to take the stage, Carvalho began a long
trawl through the haunts of ambiguous Barcelona, the
Barcelona of more than two sexes. He soon got bored
with the 'leather boys', with their leather jackets, their
jeans, their thick moustaches and the short haircuts
that they sported as they exhibited extremes of
masculinity in bars such as Chap, La Luna and El
Ciervo, with their red kerchiefs and their clinking
keyrings, an anthropological leftover of the New York

gay scene of the nineteen-seventies. No. Lebrun wouldn't have stuck with this particular spectacle for too long. It was a museum-piece.

He transferred himself to more modern gay hangouts, like the Strasse or the Greasse, where the clients were principally homosexuals who had turned the art of dressing into an adventure in expressivity, an eclectic personal language, a résumé of all the arts known to man. They were like living architectures. He began to feel nervous. While he was doing the rounds of north Barcelona, Lebrun could well have been going round the south, or vice-versa; they could end up spending the whole night crossing each other's paths, and all the time Claire's account with Contreras would be earning interest.

The principal clientele in the Divertidoh consisted of biologically unequal couples: well-heeled middle-aged father figures and young men in their prime, making eyes at the forty-something voyeurs who went to test their secret desires. In the Divertidoh, Carvalho struck up conversation with a man, an accomplice in voyeurism, a harassed business executive with five too many whiskies inside him.

'The joint's lively tonight.'

'It's always the same. And they're always the same crowd, too.'

'Do you come here often?'

'Don't get me wrong, friend.'

'I'm not getting you wrong.'

'If you're looking for a date, you're talking to the wrong man. I come to look. I like coming here. The best thing about this place is watching the people in it.'

'You're a man after my own heart. I get so much entertainment out of watching people that I don't even have time for television.'

'Put it there.'

He offered his hand, and Carvalho shook it accordingly.

'I come here once a week. I watch, I take it in, I remember, and it enables me to keep up with the way the world is going. They're all regulars here.'

'Is this the "in" place these days?'

'Not at all. The in place these days is Martin's Bar, but it starts later. You get all kinds there. It's like a zoo. All shapes and sizes.'

Carvalho decided to ditch his interlocutor, and waited for the man to get the hint. But he didn't. He put his hand on Carvalho's arm and offered to buy him a drink.

'A whisky would do me. But it has to be malt. When I'm paying I drink malt, and I don't see why I should do any different just because you're paying.'

'Put it there. I like your style. Direct, straight to the point.'

'A Knockando, please.'

'I've got eight- or twelve-year,' the barman informed them.

'The twelve-year for my friend,' said the executive, without a trace of hesitation.

'It's the whisky that the British royal family drink,' Carvalho observed, and his drinking partner looked interested.

'Just goes to show that kings and queens know a thing or two.'

'That Queen Elizabeth looks like she's been on a few binges in her time.'

'And that fat little princess too. Whisky's very good for you, you know. You piss it all out.'

'Will you be staying here long?'

'As long as the fancy takes me. I've got a wife and four children waiting at home.'

'Would you happen to have seen a couple of people passing through, a man with no eyelashes, accompanied by a dark-skinned, younger man, who looks like he might be Italian or Greek?'

'Definitely not. I would have noticed them. This whisky's really good; I'm going to have to write down the name. You know how to live, friend. I'm just a work-horse, and I don't know how to live. Seeing gays once a week is the only pleasure I get.'

'Where did you get this curious hobby?'

'From my father.'

'Was he a voyeur too?'

'No. He was a very proper person. Opus Dei. Communion every day, that sort of thing. He used to tell me: "I'd rather any son of mine was a communist, or a separatist, than a queer." He used to say it all the time, and it made me very curious about gays. It's a shame I can't write, because if I could I might write a scientific treatise on it. After all the years I've been watching them, I could set out a zoological and botanical classification of homosexuals. I know the scene inside out. Do you write?'

'I can sign my name.'

'That's the most important part. If you know how to sign your name, you're halfway there.'

'What's your line of business?'

'Travelling salesman. Canned foodstuffs from Galicia. The best sardines and the best cockles that you'll eat in town will have passed through my hands. Give me your address, and I'll send you a selection which will last you for a month of Sundays.'

Carvalho gave him a business card which had his office address on.

'A private detective, eh? Something told me that you had an interesting job. Between you and me we could write a novel. Have you tried the gents' toilet? Don't get me wrong, but doing the rounds of bars like this is like doing the rounds of salons in the best society. Where you'll find the truth about these people is in the men's toilets and in the cinemas. Do you know the area around the Arenas cinema? First-rate for that sort of thing, and the toilets at the Boulevard Rosa are interesting too, in their way. If I had a map, I could do you a fascinating itinerary, an itinerary which has taken me years and years of experience to compile, but without getting my feet wet, let's be clear about that. I'm not the sort to go with men. I know this game inside out — I'm not like other men who go round acting macho like they're God's gift to the world, claiming that the nearest they've ever come to gays is at the movies.'

Carvalho was beginning to be bored by the businessman.

'Don't you ever worry that one of your clients might see you here?'

'My clients wouldn't be seen dead in a place like this. They'd be terrified of getting AIDS even from drinking a tonic here. People have lost their sense of adventure. Not me, though. I like a bit of adventure. If they took away my little safety valve, it'd be like castrating me.'

Carvalho couldn't decide whether to do the decent thing and buy a second round, or whether to get shot of the man. He finally opted for the latter. After all, the man had offered the drink of his own free will.

'I have to get off home.'

'You got a wife waiting too?'

'Three. I'm a Mormon.'

He left the businessman swimming in a sea of cultural confusion and unsure as to whether being a Mormon was some kind of sexual aberration or whether it was in some way related with the Moonies. He was no youngster, but he evidently belonged to the generation of the ignorant who had never read Karl May and who would therefore never know what a Mormon was, or where Salt Lake City was either. Carvalho wandered aimlessly, absorbed in reflections on the art of wholesome literature, until the time came to go to Martin's Bar — a bar that was effectively a showcase for Barcelona's gay scene, and another haystack for him to go hunting in to find the needle that was Lebrun, the stupid and arrogant Lebrun who had chosen to write him off as if by ignoring him he could erase what had happened on the night in question. He passed by the office to do justice to the food that

Biscuter had prepared for him, and which the day's circumstances had turned into supper. The little man was dressed in his Sunday suit, fast asleep in front of a small television which was fruitlessly transmitting a documentary on Luis Buñuel. Carvalho didn't switch it off, for fear that the silence would wake his assistant. He ate standing in the kitchen. Suddenly an alarm clock rang in the office, and by the time he went to switch it off Biscuter was already awake, obsessively glued to the TV.

'All very interesting, this, boss. Do you know Buñuel?'

'No. Why should I know him?'

'Because you know just about everyone and everything. What does he do?'

'Cultural hooliganism.'

'Well fancy that . . .'

'And what about the girl, Biscuter?'

'Are you referring to señorita Beba?'

'Is there any other girl, Biscuter?'

'All under control. The alarm clock. My suit. I'm on my way out to follow her now. Didn't you say she was a night bird?'

'That was a very good meal you cooked there, Biscuter.'

'I did it for midday, and it's not so good when it's warmed up. The trouble is, I never know where I am with you . . .'

'Hasn't anybody rung?'

'Who are you referring to, boss? When you ask me if anybody's rung, it usually means you're asking whether someone in particular has rung.'

'The French people from the other day. Him or her.'

'No, neither of them. Charo rang, though.'

'Charo.'

The mention of her name did something to him, and he was sorry to discover that what it did was to irritate him.

'What kind of hooliganism did you mean, about Buñuel?'

'He puts dead donkeys in pianos.'

'Jesus, boss, it's true what they say about Spaniards — they're a weird bunch. What's he hoping to achieve by that, putting dead donkeys in pianos?'

'It was a dream.'

'Oh well, that's another matter. All sorts of strange things happen in dreams. OK, I'm off after señorita Brando.'

What did Biscuter dream about at nights? What heights did he reach in his dreams? Carvalho suddenly found himself in a corner of his own memory which chilled his heart almost to the point of pain. When his mother had died, it had been after several years of illness during which she had barely been able to speak. His father had told him that at night she used to talk in her sleep. He would listen. And when she talked in her sleep it had never even occurred to him to make a note of those messages which the woman was incapable of extracting from the depths of her soul during the day. Man is a rational animal who has remorse, and who actually delights in building remorse, slowly, in accumulating things that he's going to regret at a later date — words, actions, silences like the ones that were piling up in his relationship with Charo. For a moment he thought of giving up chasing after Claire's shadow and leaving her to her fate, in the assumption that she was strong enough to handle the world, with her straight back and those translucent, geological eyes. But what would be left of the relationship between men and women were it not for the self-delusion of protection? What would be the point of that harsh struggle between two animals that are spiritually such enemies, were it not mediated by the convention that one of them is fragile and the other is her protector? This was the reason why he had been so hurt by the cold way in which Claire had expelled him from her encounter with Alekos. It was also the reason why, despite his theories about remorse, despite his guilty conscience as regards Charo — because his longing for Claire was the genuine article — despite all this, he found himself in the street heading for Martin's Bar, continuing along the Via Crucis of his search for Lebrun, which was also a search for Claire. And he met himself standing outside the door of Martin's, as if running into somebody surprising that he'd not known before. He was almost trampled underfoot by four young men who were laughing at some secret joke and shouting as they went by:

'Best put your condom on before you go in there!'

Inside you could see nothing, but there was a curious smell of cheap sweat and expensive cologne, or maybe it was the other way round, cheap cologne and expensive sweat. The dominant colour was black — on the ground floor because it was painted black, and on the upper floor because the place was in total darkness and the dark was a willing accomplice to the octopuses who were massaging some very secret human flesh up there. He suddenly felt very despondent, because it wasn't the sort of place for Georges Lebrun. Lebrun liked to watch, and here you couldn't see a thing, except when the lighted glow of a cigarette gave you the chance to peek into corners that were packed with pornography — now you see it, now you don't — like a slide show operated by a sadist's hand. It was his last, childish opportunity, and he continued with his search at the risk of appearing like a Peeping Tom who was living dangerously.

'Well well, it's Little Red Riding Hood — who are you looking for, love?'

'My grandma.'

'We only get grandads here, dear.'

For a moment he thought of jumping up on a table and shouting Lebrun's name, but if he did there was a distinct risk that the bar's heavies would turn him into a human football and kick him out onto the street. Shit, he thought, and said as much out loud. Shit. Shit. Shit. And at that point he gave up, partly because there was no obvious sign of Lebrun, and partly because it was becoming increasingly obvious that this bar wasn't at all the sort of place where he was likely to find the Frenchman. He felt a primal sense of relief from the street and the cool of the autumn air. If he wasn't hiding away in a hotel somewhere, where was Georges Lebrun likely to be? The night was beginning to give way to early morning, and the time of Lebrun's appointment was getting so close that it seemed almost pointless trying to gain a few hours. Contreras must have been asleep at that moment, and the corpse of a Greek drug addict was hardly going to be giving him sleepless nights. But he was wrong. A shadow suddenly materialized at his elbow with the aid of the neon sign outside Martin's Bar, and his nostrils were assailed by a whiff of cheap cigar smoke. The man smiled. He looked like one of Contreras's minions, sure enough.

'You hang out in some pretty weird places, Carvalho.'

'I thought you were supposed to be incognito when you follow people.'

'Not always. I got tired of following you.'

'You must have got bored because I spent the whole afternoon in Plaza de Catalunya feeding the pigeons.'

'What pigeons?'

The way he reacted made it obvious that he hadn't been following him all afternoon, but had probably only connected with him at the moment that he'd emerged from his office.

'Time for little owls to return to their nests, and for me to go home.'

'Does the "little owls" refer to me?'

'No. It's a Castilian saying.'

He took advantage of the arrival of a taxi which had just dumped two men outside the bar, and climbed in, leaving the policeman in a state of surprised solitude. He watched through the rear window, and noted that he wasn't reacting. On the other hand there was no guarantee that he wasn't working as part of a pair, and that the other one wasn't still on his heels, so in a moment of inspiration he told the cabbie to take him to

Horta. There he waited for a while, alone in the sleeping city, and when another cab came along, he instructed the driver to take him to Plaza Medinaceli. It had occurred to him that maybe Lebrun had decided to try another session chez Dotras, seeing that he'd been so fascinated the last time by the nostalgic spectacle of the orphans of May '68. As the cab drove along, the few distant lights of Vallvidrera and Tibidabo filled him with a strong desire, a longing, to go home. He let himself be borne passively along to his destination, and once he hit the street he trudged wearily along thoroughfares that were damp from the morning breeze coming off the sea, until he arrived at the alley where Dotras's studio was located. All the doors were wide open, including the door to the studio, where the best part of twenty people were fast asleep, with Leonard Cohen playing in the background. It was then that he saw Lebrun, sitting on a heap of cushions, looking thoughtful and melancholic, with Mitia at his side, absolutely fast asleep, and all of the rest of them asleep too, willingly hurling one more night down the dark well of nothingnesses. Lebrun saw him at once, but he didn't bat an eyelid, and without too much effort Carvalho repressed the urge to go over to him. He was tired, and suspected that the outcome of all his searching would turn out not to have been worth the effort he'd put into it. He served himself a glass of Cuba Libre from where it had been prepared in a large jug, having first asked permission from a Dotras who was embalmed in the aroma of the joints that he had smoked. With a glass in one hand he headed for the kitchen in search of something to eat. Behind the dividing curtain he found señora Dotras, with her half-naked breasts hanging over the kitchen stove, her skirts raised, and her buttocks being rent asunder by the moist, purple, battering-ram of a young man who was not quite up to the job. But he screwed the boss's wife with a professionalism straight out of a porno film, and all the while she moaned quietly, with her straggly grey hair hanging over the half-empty saucepans. Carvalho could have withdrawn politely, but he decided to stay and appreciate the perfection of the scenario. It had been a savage, spontaneous sexual congress, reminiscent of communists, younger than himself, at the end of the nineteen-sixties. In those days people used to fuck with a naturalness that we will not see again in our times, and señora Dotras was all of a sudden queen for a day — doubtless additionally stimulated by the fact that it was taking place in her kitchen, and not a thousand miles from where her husband was floating in his cloud of remembrance and forgetting. The scene had a certain fundamental beauty, and might have brought tears to Carvalho's eyes. He almost felt like going up to the woman to stroke her hair and wish her an eternal orgasm, but fortunately a profound sense of the ridiculous prevailed, and he left the kitchen as if he had seen nothing. Lebrun was watching him as he emerged, and Carvalho didn't give him the satisfaction of going over to him immediately. In fact he sought the opposite corner of the room, and busied himself in the extremely slow consumption of his Cuba Libre. Lebrun raised his own glass in a distant toast, and lifted his head to check, or watch over, or protect the sleeping form of Mitia. The bold warrior emerged from the kitchen with a dish of rice salad in one hand and the other hand checking for the last time that his fly was done up; seconds later señora Dotras appeared with a renewed lightness in her step, and her sing-song voice announcing *urbi et orbi* that there was still enough food left to feed a regiment. But her words hung uselessly among the vapours of the room. Normality had been restored, and she returned to her kitchen alcove. Minutes passed, and Carvalho began to wonder who would be the first to put himself in the firing line. In the end it was Lebrun, who, having checked once more to see that Mitia was sleeping, got up with a lightness that Carvalho envied and crossed the room. They sat in silence while Lebrun finished the joint that he had in his hand, seeing that Carvalho had declined his offer of a smoke.

'Were you out looking for me, or is this a chance encounter?'

'I wouldn't usually be seen dead in a place like this. This is only the second time I've ever been here.'

'To tell the truth, I found it more attractive the first time. The music's different, but all the rest is the same.'

'It's never a good idea to come back for more.'

'One should never force circumstances.'

This was said rather pointedly, and Carvalho came back at him:

'You think you've got everything under control, but you haven't. The police have been asking me questions and I need to find some answers pretty damn quick.'

'For example?'

'Who's going to be claiming the body?'

'Easily solved. At this precise moment, in Paris, Claire, under her real name, will be contacting the French consulate here. She will have received word that a body has been discovered, and this information will have come from a friend who lives in Barcelona and who read it in the papers. Once Alekos's identity has been established I shall take charge of everything. I still have a few days left in Barcelona.'

'Claire isn't really called Claire, then?'

'No. We obviously didn't want to make it too easy to identify her. But you and I might as well carry on calling her Claire.'

'You have a meeting tomorrow at the Olympic office.'

'How do you know?'

'I'm not only a guide for *Barcelona by Night*, I'm a private detective too, you know. If I were you, I wouldn't underestimate Contreras, the cop who's dealing with this case. You have to watch him — he's capable of reacting in ways that you wouldn't expect, and he's got the sting of a scorpion. He knows that there were other people involved.'

'You can give my name.'

'He's likely to find out that there was a woman with us.'

'I've got the very woman. A French mercenary, who's learned off by heart everything we did that night.'

'Claire, or whatever her name is, is presumably somewhere safe now.'

'Yes. And so am I. The one who's in biggest danger is

Mitia, and if Mitia is in danger, the whole thing could collapse. My first idea was to take him to the border, but he was so depressed and moody that I was worried about leaving him alone. It's been very hard for him ever since he left France to follow Alekos. But I suspect that once we've got the body back, things will change.'

Carvalho bit his tongue to stop himself putting the question that was on his lips and which Lebrun was expecting. The Frenchman seemed more interested in explaining the role played by Mitia in the drama, than in explaining the final unfolding of their adventure.

'He's very young, but very responsible. He had everything going for him in Paris. A year ago I managed to get him enrolled in a private school where he could catch up with his education. But Alekos held an unhealthy fascination for him, which became even stronger when he found out about his illness, so he set off to follow him, come what may. For me it was a challenge, because Mitia was my statue, and I was his Pygmalion. When I first met him he was a distrustful street kid, growing up in the shadow of Alekos and his friends and feeding on their shadows. It was on the trip to Patmos that I first developed an emotional attachment, because the boy has something very deep about him, an innate touch of class.'

'So in other words there were three of you on Patmos.'

'Yes, Alekos, Mitia, and myself.'

'Was Mitia Alekos's partner, or yours?'

'Why did he necessarily have to be anyone's partner? Try to be more sophisticated, please. He was our creation. Alekos understood him in his way, and I in mine. Alekos's position was the desperation of an "other" who could never feel at home in any country, while I, for my part, was engaged in creating a statue out of Mitia.'

'And Claire . . .'

'Poor Claire . . .'

Poor Claire. There was a subtle, irritating note of condescension behind Lebrun's words. Poor Claire.

'She reacted like a hysterical woman. Something or someone was trying to take Alekos from her, and she couldn't bear that. I was her neighbour, and had a sporadic relationship with her. What Claire didn't know was that I was gradually beginning to see more and more of Alekos, separately. And it was through that relationship that I met Mitia.'

'So each of you was lying to me in your own way. You concealed your relationship with Alekos for as long as you could, until the Patmos story came up, and you never said anything about Mitia. And she never told me that she knew that Alekos was about to die.'

'Well she certainly did. When Alekos left Paris, he was mortally ill, and in my opinion he acted irresponsibly in taking Mitia with him. From that moment, both Claire and I began looking for him, each of us with our separate motives. She wanted to be sure that Alekos hadn't run off with another woman or another man, and I needed to know that Mitia was safe and that I could get him back in one piece to complete my work.'

'And when you caught up with Alekos . . .'

'He was clearly dying. It would only have been a matter of days.'

'But somebody gave him an overdose. Somebody felt moved by pity, or was it pride, to finish him off.'

'Either way, society isn't going to approve.'

'Was it pity or was it pride?'

'Perhaps both.'

'Was it you, or Claire?'

Now Lebrun smiled, as if the drama had turned itself into a slightly tedious after-dinner parlour game. The message from those lashless eyes was: 'Guess.' A sinister and curious kind of person, this, who can treat questions of life and death as if they're a game. Lebrun was still hanging fire, but Carvalho would not give him the satisfaction of begging for an answer. He sank back onto the cushions and stared up at the high ceiling with its wooden beams and the hashish vapours rising from that languid, sleeping mass of humanity. All of a sudden he heard the sound of bodies fighting, and he propped himself up on his elbows. Dotras was wrestling with one of the reclining figures, and had taken him by the scruff of the neck and was shaking him.

'Right, that's it, you shits! The show's over! This is my house! You're consuming us! You're even consuming my memories and my intelligence! You're not worth the money you pay! You sons of the great whore, go home . . . if you have homes to go to. When I was twelve years old I was already out working, and you're all just rich spoilt brats . . . At the age of twelve I was selling sweets on the streets . . . You're so mediocre and pitiful

that your memories will be painful to listen to . . .
Insipid, immature, no colour . . .'

His wife emerged abruptly from the confines of the
kitchen and as she went across to sort out her husband
she waved her hands around to indicate that everybody should leave.

'Don't go upsetting yourself, Papa.'

'Look how the bastards have left the place.'

'Papa . . .'

The woman buried the man's head between her arms
and breasts and gestured behind his back to indicate
that the rest of them should leave. Some of them were
still sleeping and were in no condition to act on her
message. The rest of them began filing out towards the
exit, as the lady of the house reminded them that the
night's festivities were not for free.

'Those of you who haven't paid, leave your money on
that ceramic Llorens Artigas dish by the door. You,
Carlet, you never paid . . . I'm watching you . . .'

This last was said to the same person who had been
shafting her in the kitchen minutes previously — a hard
woman, this — while all the time she cradled her
husband's head in her arms as he wept quietly to
himself. Mitia sensed that there was some special
relationship between Lebrun and Carvalho, even
though he had not recognized the detective as one of
the people who had been present on Alekos's last night,
nor had he been able to hear the content of the two
men's conversation. When they reached the street
outside, the file of exiles banished from chez Dotras
began to disintegrate, and by the end the only group of

any substance left was the threesome comprising Carvalho, Lebrun and Mitia.

'This gentleman is the detective who helped us find you.'

Suspicion instantly filled Mitia's dark eyes, and he held back a couple of paces to allow the two men to proceed with their private discussion.

'Despite everything, it was an unforgettable night, and not just for the reason you're thinking. That was simply a detail, a logical conclusion of a prolonged flight and a long search. I found the journey itself — the actual search — beautiful. First there was Dotras and the enterprise that he's constructed on the ruins of memory. Then all those warehouses, those factories... like archeological remains fleetingly reoccupied by transient, ethereal industries of dreams . . . sculptors, photographers . . .'

'All at death's door.'

Lebrun didn't appreciate the crudeness of Carvalho's interjection. He shut his eyes:

'You Spaniards are too tragic. What I remember from that night is all the Icarias, and all you remember is the sordid sight of a syringe and the death of a man who was already at death's door anyway.'

And he initiated an ill-humoured silence which lasted until he finally decided that the time had come to end both the story of what had happened and his relationship with Carvalho.

'It was Claire. She would never have allowed me to do it for her. Alekos was hers. And her property rights weren't being threatened by another woman, or by another man, but by the approach of death. Claire had the injection already prepared in her handbag, from the moment we arrived in Barcelona. Do you remember the way she had her arms folded over that bag of hers, the way she was holding it so closely? As if she was protecting an anti-Eucharist. There she was carrying all her pity and all her pride in Alekos.'

'And him?'

'I don't know what they talked about. You saw for yourself the way she took him over as soon as she saw him and you and I were surplus to requirements. What I do know is that Alekos allowed her to give the injection without protesting, and, I would say, with a certain sense of relief. Mitia realized what was going on only when it was too late, and threw a tantrum. But that passed. For him, life is about to begin.'

He paused abruptly and held out his hand to Carvalho.

'I imagine that you've received my cheque. In addition, I would like to offer my thanks and say that it has been a pleasure.'

Carvalho shook the hand that was offered, and watched Lebrun as he wandered off up the Ramblas with one arm round the shoulders of his young Greek. The detective decided to go down the Ramblas and do a bit of office work to make up for the pitiful amount he'd done in the past few days. He turned his head a couple of times to look up the Ramblas, to watch the couple gradually blend and finally disappear into the last shadows on the Rambla de las Flores and the few bystanders who were still out and about. He put on a deliberately sour look so as to preclude any possibility of having to strike up tedious dialogues with pathetic dope dealers in their cheap run-fast-when-you-need-to trainers, but found himself accosted by a dealer who must have been on the verge of bankruptcy; the man came towards him, but then something in Carvalho's eyes — perhaps the possibility that he was armed — advised him to keep his distance. When the detective arrived at his office it took him a moment or two to remember why Biscuter was not in his camp bed. He had raised him to the rank of aide de camp, and by now he would be amazing nocturnal Barcelona with his cast-iron shoulder pads and his baleful eyes. It was years since Carvalho had last experienced the sensation of being all alone in his own office, and he heightened the sensation by turning out the lights. He sank into his swivel chair, put his feet up on the table, took his newly rescued torch out of his jacket pocket, let it feel him caressing it, and just before he went to tuck it into its drawer he pressed the button and out came the wonder of its light. He used it to probe first the four corners of the room and then Biscuter's route to his den, and finally his own face, making himself look like a ghost by shining it up from his chin. He tried putting its illumin- ated dioptric eye next to his eye and then into his mouth, and then he switched it off abruptly and tossed it to the back of a large drawer. He listened as it rolled around inside and enjoyed the company of the gradu- ally subsiding noise. He was fighting off anxiety, or maybe trying to remember how he could summon it up, when there was the sound of a key in the door and there on the doorstep was the silhouette of Biscuter, faintly lit by the dim light on the landing.

'It's me, Biscuter.'

'Is that you, boss? At this time of night?'

Biscuter turned the light on, and Carvalho was able to take a leisurely look at his old companion, with his good-as-new twenty-year-old suit and a tie that looked as if it had been bought for his first communion.

'How did it go?'

'Amazing, boss! If you're not too tired, I'll tell you.'

His trusty shield-bearer went and sat in the chair that was normally reserved for clients, and prepared him- self to give a lengthy account of his comings and goings in pursuit of the Brando girl. He took a small pad of squared paper from his pocket and began his report in a slight Puerto Rican accent, in imitation of the imported North American films which are dubbed into Spanish in Puerto Rico.

'Thursday, 2230 hours. BB leaves house, taking advantage of the onset of night.'

'At that time of night, in autumn, it would hardly have been the onset of night . . .'

But Biscuter chose not to listen. He proceeded with the saga of how he had followed her around various bars, restaurants, discotheques . . .

'No drugs?'

'Not for the moment, no.'

There was no point in his continuing with his useless inventory of comings and goings, except that all of a sudden he said something which caught Carvalho's attention.

'Friday, 0215. BB leaves KGB's. At dead of night. The city is sleeping. Makes her way to the Nick Havanna Bar. Make contact with BB . . .'

'Come again, Biscuter . . .'

'Make contact with BB.'

'You do realize that once you make contact with her, you won't be able to follow her again? From now on she's going to recognize you.'

'I'm sorry, boss. The trouble is, she came over to me and started asking me all sorts of questions. She was worse than my doctor. I had to tell her all about my life. And she started saying: "Oh you poor thing, you poor thing." I felt terrible — I never realized that I've had such a terrible life. She gave me this book.'

Peter Pan. Carvalho was at a loss for words. Biscuter too.

'What was I supposed to do, boss? Should I have just made my excuses and left? She's a great girl. She invited me to go up to her house, but I thought I'd better not. She paid for the drinks, boss. And she gave me the book, too.'

Brando Senior listened to Carvalho's extensive but pointless report, in which he made no mention of Biscuter's involvement. He appreciated his work. You could see this in the way he listened carefully to what the detective had to say, as if he was well aware that behind each ritual movement in the 'boy follows girl' saga there lay a possible second reading. Carvalho actually had nothing to sell at this point. When the detective finished speaking, Brando pressed him for some sort of conclusion.

'In other words   '

'The circle is closing.'

'I'm glad to hear it.'

'I've kept a note of all her regular itineraries. There are five or six of them, and she improvises on them, depending on her mood. The moment she departs from one of them, then we know we're onto something, we know that something is about to happen.'

'Very good, Carvalho. Slow but sure. I can tell you that because I'm a man who likes to call a spade a spade.'

Carvalho's manner with Brando Junior was radically

different. He went over the same ground that he had covered with the father, but in a tone of voice that was less lyrical, more enunciatory, better suited to a thirty-year-old male who had lived through what had been bad times for lyric and epic poetry.

'Is that all?'

'Yes.'

'It's not much, is it? You haven't even tried forcing the situation. My sister could carry on like this for months on end, and one day, when you're not looking, she's going to slip her leash. You need to provoke a situation where something's going to happen. In business theory this is called increasing the supply in order to stimulate demand. You follow?'

He thought of telling him to get lost, but then he reflected that hard times were probably just around the corner, and so decided against. Brando Junior was not about to get any better; in fact he would probably get worse. But one had to develop one's relations with these mutants, in order to master their language as a first step to gaining mastery of their souls. Both he and Biscuter had got egg on their faces in their relationship with the girl, but he decided that he could continue to use Biscuter as the vanguard, exposed to view, since his role as an infatuated follower of Tinkerbell would be perfectly plausible.

'If she happens to rumble you, just pretend to be nervous.'

'Don't worry, boss. I won't need to pretend.'

'More than usual, though. As if you're a teenager who's just been found out by the girl he's following.'

'Are you saying that I should let her think that I'm in

love with her . . . Open my heart to her? All right, fair enough, I will . . . I'll say: "Ever since the first time I saw you going out, taking advantage of the onset of night . . ." Oh hell, I said the bit about the onset of night again . . .'

'No. Go ahead — tell her that you've been following her ever since the first time you saw her going out of her house taking advantage of the onset of night . . . That way she'll think you've been following her since June.'

'So what happens then, when I've declared myself, boss? I wouldn't want to create false hopes.'

The tactical choice was clear. Biscuter would be the vanguard and he himself would bring up the rear. Brando Junior was right. He had lost his capacity for initiative. He didn't entirely trust the new system, so for that reason the first few days saw Biscuter following Beba and Carvalho following Biscuter, and when his assistant came to some particularly interesting cross-roads, he would laboriously retrace his steps back to the office to tell his boss, by which time Beba would have taken flight. Finally Carvalho decided that for a couple of days he would stay on duty in the office, and Biscuter would simply ring in whenever he noticed Beba doing anything out of the ordinary. This eventually occurred during the night of the second day of the new system, when Biscuter rang him in an agitated state from a public phone down the Ramblas, which Carvalho could clearly see from the window of his office. As if he was calling from the other end of town or the other end of the world Biscuter was shouting.

'Do me a favour, I can see you from the window here, Biscuter, no need to shout!'

'Boss, the girl's gone . . .'

'Where's she gone?'

'Here, over at the side, in Arco del Teatro, and she's talking with the dealers, boss . . .'

'I'll be down straight away.'

He went down the stairs three at a time, and was surprised to discover reserves of elasticity that he never knew he had. When he reached the street, he had to stop to get his breath back and to assume a normal walking pace so as not to alarm the zombies of the night who were out trawling the city's rubbish bins, and the other nightwalkers who occupied the Ramblas in the hope of finding an easy pick-up among the city's shipwrecked wayfarers. Biscuter was standing next to the bar, which specialized in the sale of cazalla *eau de vie*, and had the curious look of a Chinese spy awaiting the knife-blow that is going to deprive him of his last breath. And there . . . there was Beba, advancing towards them, her body illuminated by the dirtiest street lamps in the whole world and pursued by the eyes of the inhabitants of this social leper colony. Carvalho surprised Biscuter by sending him back to the office.

'But it's just starting to get interesting, boss!'

'I'll tell you what happens later.'

Beba had parked her car at the bottom of the statue to Pitarra. A couple of traffic wardens were beginning to sniff round the vehicle, but they must have taken a fancy to her, because they gave her a military salute, and then began making suggestive comments behind her back. Carvalho got into his car and crossed the paved pedestrian zone of the Ramblas in order to turn the car round and tuck it in behind Beba's. The manoeuvre was so illegal that it took the two policemen a moment before they reacted, and they barely had time to pull out their fixed-penalty pads and insult him before he was off down the road. The girl was heading for the city's heights, and when she reached Diagonal, instead of driving home through the residential area of Can Caralleu she drove down Paseo de la Bonanova and parked in front of the villa where her mother spent her days abusing the bearers of some of the city's most distinguished surnames. She leapt out of her car and tripped across to the main door. She must have had a key, because she didn't bother to ring and went straight in as if she owned the place. Carvalho began hunting around in his glove compartment to find the most suitable lock-pick for his purpose, but the house alarm was not switched on — the girl's arrival had evidently been expected and she simply pulled the door to behind her. This meant that Carvalho only needed a credit card to get in. Once inside, he had to duck back to avoid finding himself face to face with the strange procession that emerged from the office. First came the smiling ex-gymnast, with Beba pushing him in his wheelchair, and next came the mother, like an enthusiastic bridesmaid, ushering them down the corridor with flailing arms and singing out loud:

'This is going to be your night of glory, Sebastian!'

Sebastian tried to urge the wheelchair onwards with

movements of his buttocks and his feet pushed against the footrest; he was distributing lavish smiles to his wife and to Beba as she manouevred his wheelchair. The mother then struck up with the *Marseillaise* and waved her arms under Sebastian's nose, as if conducting him, when she reached the line.

'Le jour de gloire est arrivé!'

The wheelchair and its contents were wheeled into the main hall of the gym, where the mother proceeded to set the scene, setting up a little table and a stool, and pulling the gymnastic rings along a metal rail until they were hanging over the invalid's head. Sebastian looked up, and was wide-eyed with excitement as he looked at the rings hanging above him. Beba opened her handbag, took out an envelope and poured part of its contents onto the table; at the same time she received from her mother's hands a silver tube which she used to mark out lines of white powder on the table top. The mother followed the operation with her nose slightly raised and her whole body leaning over to watch what the girl was doing, and turning her head every so often to give Sebastian a look of complicity. There were now three lines of cocaine on the polished surface of the table, and Beba handed the invalid the silver tube. He took it as if it were an instrument of religious devotion, placing it up one nostril with one hand and using the other to block the other nostril. He took three good snorts, each followed by a raising of his head to enable the dust to reach his most sensitive mucuses, and then his fingers groped greedily at the remaining specks of dust that were still on the table top and put them into his open mouth with a grimace like a hungry duck. The women moved to the other side of the table, and Sebastian looked at them defiantly as he prepared for the second part of the spectacle which was about to begin. First he pushed the wheelchair away and stood there, on the floor, on his own, with his legs slightly apart and his arms moving around to keep his balance. Having once got his balance, he put his legs together, then flexed them, and finally, with the assistance of the women, climbed up onto the stool which enabled him to reach the rings.

'Right, that's it — go on!' he ordered, and Beba and her mother hastened to remove the stool. Sebastian raised himself and then pushed the rings away from him with trembling arms until he hung there, looking like Christ on the cross, with his feet together, his head held high, the muscles in his neck looking like they were about to burst, and the women applauding the invalid gymnast enthusiastically.

'Better than ever!'

'Wonderful, Sebas . . .!'

Carvalho withdrew quietly, and on the way back to renew his acquaintance with his house he wondered how he was going to write up his report for Brando Senior, or how he would explain to Brando Junior that he had decided against taking up the job as Beba's guardian angel. 'Keep back, lady, no one is going to catch me and make me a man,' Peter Pan had said at the moment when he definitively decided that he was never going to grow up. When Carvalho arrived home, he went looking for the James M. Barrie book in order to burn it, but he couldn't find it. Then he slowly recalled the personal circumstances in which he had burned it, ten or eleven years previously. It had been after a heavy drinking session, which had led him to rediscover the childish anger he had felt at the fact that Wendy wasn't able to fly and would never be able to share in Peter Pan's destiny. He was going to have to buy another copy so that he could burn it a second time, and from the flames he would conjure up the innocent nakedness of Beba, although his courage would fail at the prospect of asking her to do him a favour or two and help make his own invalidity more bearable. But then Carvalho came back to his senses, and he heard himself say: 'She screwed us, the little angel!' And he found himself putting a face to the naked, unveiled goddess, and it changed from Beba's features to Claire's, and then from Claire's back to Beba's, and he was annoyed that señorita Beba was able to encroach on the space which he would have preferred to keep for Claire alone. The scene of the invalid on drugs could be seen either way — as beautiful, or as sordid, depending on how you looked at it, and the same went for the image of Claire finishing off Alekos. There are women in this world who swallow you whole.

Dear Pepe,
For some weeks now you'll have heard about my feelings from Biscuter, because I've been using him as a handkerchief for my tears. I've only ever called you at

the office, because I wanted to leave you free to decide if you wanted to phone back or not. I knew that phoning you at home would be putting you on the spot, and I didn't want to hear you sounding annoyed with me because I was ringing. I'm not going to ask you, like I have so many times before, what's happening to us, Pepe, because I don't want to hear your answer; and I'm not going to ask you to take me to the pictures, or out to dinner, or up to your house in Vallvidrera so that I can make love with my favourite client. You've never avoided me as much as this before. You'll have to forgive me, but I've followed you several times, and I've seen you fluttering around a couple of very pretty girls. According to what Biscuter has told me, one of them is French, and that makes sense because that's the kind of woman you'd probably go for, because you never know if they're coming or going, and you like unsolved mysteries. The other girl worries me more, because she's only a kid. But anyway, I've long since got over being amazed at the stupid things that men of your age can get up to when they fancy themselves as vampires and think that sucking young blood is going to rejuvenate them. I wouldn't say that you're in the same class of idiot, and maybe you're going through a bad period, so bad that you don't need me, Pepe, and it makes me very sad to think that, very sad, and I just cry all the time. Biscuter tells me that the young girl is just another professional case, but I can tell from his voice that he's noticed as well. It's as if something is happening to you, something deep, very deep, very very hidden, as if what little heart you had left in you has finally died. I've just

*had to go and renew my National Identity Card, and I
had no choice but to read my date of birth. For years
now I've been putting four sorts of cream on my face in
winter, and as many as six in summer – creams, not
'pomades' as you like to call them. My make-up has
changed over the years; once it was 'aquarelle', as you
used to describe it, but now it's oil paint. Beneath my
creams and my rouges, time is creeping up. I feel it in the
way I move, and I see it in the things I like to remember,
and the things I long for and would like to happen.
These are bad times for an ageing prostitute. I feel
caught in the middle between the complete wrecks and
the tall, good-looking twenty-year-olds who are good for
nothing much more than putting on condoms for their
clients, and talking high-class, which they are not. My
regular clients are all getting older; they're starting to
prefer a normal life, and their wives have turned into
well-preserved grandmothers by now. The men are
starting to be scared for their children, and their
grandchildren, with the whole of their lives still ahead
of them. Nowadays they never say an unkind word
about their wives; quite the opposite – the few times that
they come to see me, they're always saying nice things
about them. They want me to call them by the same pet
names that they use. They're scared of their wives,
because they know that women age better than men
and will outlive them. Sometimes they pay me without
having sex, and on those occasions they don't leave a tip.
Symptoms, Pepe, symptoms that all this is coming to an
end, and I shall be turning fifty soon, more painted than
ever, with more creams, and waiting by the phone for*

them to call me, and for you not to call me. I don't think it would have been any better if I'd told you all this to your face. I can see it very clearly. Better that it just stays in writing, and that you remember me as I was, as we were, the last time that you came round to take me out to cure me of the blues, or our trip to Paris, at last, last spring. Do you remember that trip to Paris, Pepe? Do you remember how much I was talking, and how little you were talking? Do you remember how happy I was, and how you weren't? I suppose what I'm getting at is that I'm running out of things to say to you. I've decided to leave. I've been offered an opportunity, not particularly brilliant, but still an opportunity, in Andorra. An old client of mine has a hotel up there, and he's bored with having to go up and down all the time to keep an eye on things. He's asked me to supervise the hotel for him. Make sure they're not robbing him, smile at the clients in reception, wander around among the tables at dinner time and ask everyone if everything's going all right. Life up there is a bit boring, but he says it's very healthy, and he doesn't know how I can bear to breathe the shit that we have to breathe in this Barrio Chino, even though they're supposed to be opening it up now. Even more, he says he doesn't know how I can bear the shame of the barrio. It's as if the city keeps it as a showcase for every kind of human ruination. Anyway, I think I've made up my mind. I'm going to take him up on his offer. The money side of it isn't bad. Food, lodging, a hundred thousand clear per month, and the kind of treatment that only you have ever given me – as between equals, from person to person. Biscuter knows

Andorra well, from the days when he used to go up there stealing cars for his weekend jaunts and smuggling bottles of whisky and Duralex dinner services. Biscuter hasn't told me either yes or no, but you, with your silence, you've told me yes. I would have liked to write to you about our good times, which there have certainly been, through the years of our relationship, but this has been such an effort for me to write that I would prefer just to take them with me as memories. I don't want you to feel guilty. When all's said and done, I have always known that you've listened to me so as not to have to listen to me, and that you never feel guilty anyway. I love you.

Charo.

Biscuter had taken refuge in his little back room. Carvalho could almost hear him breathing. He'd had a hangdog look when he'd handed over Charo's letter; Carvalho was not in the mood for hangdog looks. He went out into the street, fully intending to go to Charo's house and persuade her to change her mind. However, when he arrived at the church of Santa Monica, his attention was distracted by a poster announcing an exhibition of paintings in the church, and by the sight of the Calcutta-style traffic surrounding the monument to Christopher Columbus, a pre-Olympic collapse of urban circulation resulting from the roadworks which were intended to facilitate the forthcoming Olympics. His feet strayed from the path which would have led

him to Charo's. Maybe he'd go the next day. And he
followed the last sloping bit of the Ramblas down to the
port to see if the encounter with the woman of his
dreams was really going to happen. He sensed that this
was the last time in his life that he was going to be able
to behave like an adolescent, ignoring the reality of age
as dictated by calendars and national identity cards,
and he allowed his legs to carry him down to the docks,
picking his way through the congested traffic and
keeping a wary eye on the hysterical drivers, until he
arrived at the water's edge. On the surface of the dirty
water, in among the oil slicks and the garbage on the
surface, he saw the body of Claire floating, with her
geological, translucent eyes, and that smile which
concealed as much truth as it conveyed. A smile that
was like a mist of spray. He closed his eyes, and when he
opened them again all he saw was the water, like a dirty
mirror, and the bulky outlines of boats that were so
firmly anchored that they looked as if they were set in
rock.

**Also by Manuel Vázquez Montalbán
and published by Serpent's Tail**

Murder in the Central Committee

Translated by Patrick Camiller

'A sharp wit and a knowing eye' *Sunday Times*

'Montalbán is a writer who is caustic about the powerful and tender towards the oppressed' *TLS*

'I cannot wait for other Pepe Carvalho titles to be published here. Meanwhile, make the most of *Murder in the Central Committee*' *New Statesman*

'Montalbán writes with authority and compassion — a Le Carré-like sorrow' *Publishers Weekly*

'A thriller worthy of the name: a taut, intelligent tour de force set in the shadowy minefield of post-Franco Spanish politics' Julie Burchill

'Splendid flavour of life in Barcelona and Madrid, a memorable hero in Pepe and one of the most startling love scenes you'll ever come across' *Scotsman*

The lights go out during a meeting of the Central Committee of the Spanish Communist Party — Fernando Garrido, the general secretary, has been murdered.

Pepe Carvalho, who has worked for both the Party and the CIA, is well suited to track down Garrido's murderer. Unfortunately, the job requires a trip to Madrid — an inhospitable city where food and sex is heavier than in Pepe's beloved Barcelona.

Southern Seas

Translated by Patrick Camiller

'Pepe Carvalho is a phlegmatic investigator. His greatest concern is with his stomach, but when not pursuing delicacies, he can unravel the most tangled of mysteries' *Sunday Times*

The body of Stuart Pedrell, a powerful businessman, is found in a Barcelona suburb. He had disappeared on his way to Polynesia in search of the visionary spirit of Paul Gauguin.

Who better to find the killer of a dead dreamer than Pepe Carvalho, overweight bon viveur and ex-communist? The trail for Pedrell's killer unearths a world of disillusioned lefties, graphic sex and nouvelle cuisine — major ingredients of post-Franco Spain. A tautly-written mystery with an unforgettable — and highly unusual — protagonist.

Off Side

Translated by Ed Emery

'Magical detection' *The List*

'If you haven't yet made the acquaintance of Carvalho, now's the time. He's the most original detective to come along in an age and the mix of political intrigue, Barcelona style, and Catalan cooking tips, makes for a great read' *Venue*

'Because you use your centre forward to make yourselves feel like gods who can manage victories and defeats, from the comfortable throne of minor Caesars: the centre forward will be killed at dusk.'

To revive its sagging fortunes, Barcelona FC has bought the services of Jack Mortimer, European Footballer of the Year. No sooner has Mortimer taken possession of his company Porsche than death threats start arriving. Are they a hoax, the work of a loner or are they connected to the awesome real estate speculation that is tearing Barcelona apart?

In a period of turmoil where Catalan pimps and racketeers are being hustled off the streets by crime syndicates from the Middle East, Pepe Carvalho is thinking of retirement, but the need to save the soul of his beloved Barcelona forces him to take on a case that can only end in disaster.

The Angst-Ridden Executive

Translated by Ed Emery

'More Montalbán please!' *City Limits*

Antonio Jauma, an old acquaintance, dies desperately wanting to get in touch with Pepe Carvalho. Jauma's widow has good reason to believe that her husband's death is not what it seems. And who better to investigate than Carvalho, a private eye with a CIA past and contacts with the Communist Party.

The Buenos Aires Quintet

Translated by Nick Caistor

When Pepe Carvalho's uncle asks him to find his son, Raúl, in Buenos Aires, Pepe is reluctant. All he knows about Argentina is 'tango, Maradona, and the disappeared' and he has no desire to find out more.

But family is family and soon Carvalho is in Buenos Aires, getting more caught up in Argentina's troubled past than is good for anybody. As he gets nearer to finding Raúl, he begins to realize the full impact of the traumas caused by a military junta who went so far as to kidnap the children of the political activists they tortured.

A few excellent tangos, bottles of Mendoza Cabernet Sauvignon and a sexy semiotician are no compensation for the savage brutality Carvalho experiences in his attempt to come to grips with Argentina's recent history.

Other Serpent's Tail books of interest

The Garden of Secrets

Juan Goytisolo

Twenty-eight storytellers — one for each letter in the Arabic alphabet — meet in a Marrakesh garden to tell the story of a poet, Eusebio, arrested in the early days of the Spanish Civil War. Eusebio, a friend of Garcia Lorca and his Circle, had escaped assassination and fled to North Africa.

Some tales embroider his shadowy life with stories that feature the pasha's cook, the slave-market, Aysha and the stork . . . Others want to know if Eusebio betrayed his fascist friends by confessing in a show-trial or played the shadowy role of double-agent. Is he Eugenio the World War Two black marketeer from Tangiers or Alphonse van Worden, supposed descendent of Count Potocki, doyen of Marrakesh queens with his Rolls, Philippines' chauffeur and home showings of Mary Pickford movies?

With answers that are violent, parodic and erotic, Goytisolo's storytellers question the nature of memory, history and myth. *Tristram Shandy* and *A Thousand and One Nights* are enlisted to show the chameleon nature of truth. In *The Gardens of Secrets*, Juan Goytisolo reminds us that ultimately it is fiction that is the arbiter of what really happens.

Born in Barcelona in 1931, Juan Goytisolo is Spain's greatest living writer. A bitter opponent of the Franco regime, his early novels were banned in Spain. In 1956, he moved to Paris and has since written novels, essays and two volumes of autobiography. *A Cock-Eyed Comedy, Landscapes after the Battle, Makbara, The Virtues of the Solitary Bird* and his extra-ordinary trilogy, *Marks of Identity, Count Julian* and *Juan the Landless* are also published by Serpent's Tail. Juan Goytisolo now lives in Marrakesh.

Landscapes After the Battle

Juan Goytisolo

'Juan Goytisolo is one of the most rigorous and original contemporary writers. His books are a strange mixture of pitiless autobiography, the debunking of mythologies and conformist fetishes, passionate exploration of the periphery of the West — in particular of the Arab world which he knows intimately — and audacious linguistic experiment. All these qualities feature in *Landscapes After the Battle*, an unsettling, apocalyptic work, splendidly translated by Helen Lane' Mario Vargas Llosa

'*Landscapes After the Battle* . . . a cratered terrain littered with obscenities and linguistic violence, an assault on "good taste" and the reader's notions of what a novel should be' *Observer*

'Fierce, highly unpleasant and very funny' *Guardian*

'A short exhilarating tour of the emergence of pop culture, sexual liberation and ethnic militancy' *New Statesman*

'Helen Lane's rendering reads beautifully, capturing the whimsicality and rhythms of the Spanish without sacrificing accuracy, but rightly branching out where literal translation simply does not work' *Times Literary Supplement*

Makbara

Juan Goytisolo

'. . . a comic, smiling parody that mirrors in reverse the agitation, the frenzy, the commotion of operation on the New York Stock Exchange during its frequent gales of euphoric optimism or gusts of panic, when the Dow Jones average suddenly shoots upward or suddenly tumbles amid the frantic shouts of customers, the dizzying shifts in the figures posted on the big board, the frantic clatter of the stock tickers, the rapid-fire gibberish of the professional traders . . .'

In Arabic, the word 'Makbara' refers to those parts of North African cemeteries where young couples go to get away from their elders and hang out.

A celebration of *amour fou*, *Makbara* reveals Goytisolo's deep love for Arab culture seen as sensuous and lewd in contrast to the drab sterility of the West. In a series of scenes, pastiches and travelling shots, Goytisolo exposes cultural, sexual and political oppression. The author's message, delivered in polyphonic style, is of liberation through sex which as he says 'is above all freedom'.

Praise for *Makbara*

'No one has conducted a fiercer, more rewarding battle against this esthetic and material fact of fiction's life than Juan Goytisolo. He succeeds, to the degree that anyone can — and the list of contenders is long, honorable, including Woolf, Joyce, Sterne — by putting the novel in flux' Ronald Christ

A Cock-Eyed Comedy

Juan Goytisolo

God works in mysterious ways ... and in *A Cock-Eyed Comedy*, Juan Goytisolo takes on the Spanish Catholic church.

Father Trennes, our hero, is like Virginia Woolf's Orlando, a spirit of the age moving through several centuries of history. His most recent incarnation is as a member of the conservative right wing Catholic organisation, Opus Dei, whose founder, Josemaría Escrivá, has just been canonized.

A cast of historical characters, including philosopher Roland Barthes, Jean Genet and Argentine writer Manuel Puig, meet and mingle with a host of imaginary ones in an orgiastic romp until AIDS takes its toll.

Joe Orton meets *Father Ted* in this knockabout comedy which is also a vicious satire on the darker side of the history of the church: a church with many skeletons in its closet.

'Goytisolo's extraordinary lyrical and imaginative gifts are simultaneously forceful and beguiling, and the only response is to give in to the tumultuous, hallucinatory voices' *Observer*

Dona Flor and Her Two Husbands

Jorge Amado

'Jorge Amado has been writing immensely popular novels for fifty years. His books are on a grand scale, long, lavish, highly coloured ... Amado has vigour, panache, raciness, exoticism ...' *Times Literary Supplement*

'Reading *Dona Flor and Her Two Husbands* is like having a tropical jungle of scented flowers in blazing colours explode in your face. For not only has Amado brought to life the whole teeming city of Bahia where the story is set, but he has so filled it with the musky perfume of physical love that it almost saturates the senses' *Cincinnati Enquirer*

When Dona Flor's husband dies suddenly, she forgets all his defects and remembers only his passion. Erotic nightmares haunt her. Dr Teodoro, a local pharmacist, proposes marriage and Dona Flor accepts, hoping to recapture the ecstasy she now craves.

One night, her first husband materializes naked at the foot of her bed, eager to reclaim his conjugal rights. The visit is the first of many, as Dona Flor, racked by desire but reluctant to betray the upright pharmacist, responds to the ethereal demands of her first husband.

Dona Flor and Her Two Husbands is the work of a brilliant story-teller whose love for his characters matches his powers of evocation. An epic book.

The Seven Madmen

Roberto Arlt

'If great means anything at all, then Arlt is surely a great writer . . . He is Latin America's first truly urban novelist . . . This is the power which inspired literature possesses' Martin Seymour-Smith

First published in 1929, *The Seven Madmen* perfectly captures the conflict of Argentine society, at a crucial moment in its history.

Arlt's exploration of the still mysterious city of Buenos Aires, its street slang, crowded tenements, crazy juxtapositions, and anguish are at the core of this novel. In this seething, hostile city, Erdosain wanders the streets, trying to decipher the teeming life going on behind dark doors. He searches, literally, for his soul that is causing him so much pain, wondering what it might look like.

This translation of Arlt's masterpiece makes available to English speaking audiences the work of a writer who is the founder of the contemporary Latin American novel and a giant of 20th century literature.

The Investigation

Juan José Saer

He's called 'the monster of the Bastille'. He's brutally murdered 27 elderly women in one area of Paris. Chief Inspector
Morvan is in charge of the investigation into this macabre
and sinister case: every victim seems to have invited the
killer into her home, to have enjoyed a meal, even celebrated,
before her death. And each time the killer has meticulously
bathed himself, leaving the scene of the crime without a
single fingerprint.

In Argentina meanwhile, an untitled manuscript by an
unnamed author is discovered amongst the papers of a
missing poet, known for his hatred of the novel.

The Investigation seeks to unravel two cases — one criminal,
one literary. Part police investigation, part historical account
and part novel, it shows Saer at his virtuoso best, orchestra-
ting the different layers effortlessly. Hitchcockian, blending
suspense with superb descriptions of everyday life, this is
both a crime novel and a journey into the psyche of horror.

Nobody Nothing Never

Juan José Saer

'Now he dismounts, well in the background, underneath the eucalyptus trees, and laboriously frees the horse of its reins and saddle. The perforations of light that filter through the foliage leave spots on man and horse that move when they move. The whole ground is strewn with circles of light. I take the salami out of the refrigerator, the bread out of the sack. Tilty follows my movements as he talks.

"Night before last they killed another one in Santa Rosa," he says. "That makes nine."

"Ten," I say. "Last night they killed one here in Rincón . . ." '

During a stifling Argentinian summer, a horse-killer is on the loose. Cat Garay, heir to a once-prosperous, now dilapidated family, and his lover Elisa protect a horse from certain mutilation and death. An intense sexual affair and a desultory hunt for the killer are played out on the banks of the Paraná river in an atmosphere of political anxiety and disintegration.

The haunting prose of *Nobody Nothing Never* confirms Juan José Saer's reputation as the most innovative Latin American writer of his generation.

The Lizard's Tail

Luisa Valenzuela

The lizard's tail is a whip much favoured by Latin American torturers. It gives its name to this fictional biography of López Rega, Isabel Peron's minister of social well-being who ruled Argentina through sorcery and witchcraft.

A figure of immense power and cruelty, López Rega survives all attempts by politicians and the military to overthrow him. So great is the magic of this power-crazed witchdoctor that the writer/narrator can destroy him only by removing herself: 'By erasing myself from the map, I intend to erase you. Without my biography, it will be as if you never had a life. So long, Sorcerer, *felice morte.*'

In *The Lizard's Tail*, Luisa Valenzuela re-invents language to convey the political reality of Latin America. A reality in which the very survival of writing and the writer hangs in the balance.

'To read her is to enter our reality fully, and to participate in a search for a Latin American identity which continues to enrich itself. The books of Luisa Valenzuela are our present, but they also contain much of our future; there is real sun, real love, real liberty in each of her pages' Julio Cortázar

'Luisa Valenzuela has written a wonderfully free, ingenious novel about sensuality and power, history and death, the "I" and literature. Only a Latin American could have written *The Lizard's Tail*, but there is nothing like it in contemporary Latin American literature' Susan Sontag

'Luisa Valenzuela is the heiress of Latin American fiction. She wears an opulent, baroque crown, but her feet are naked' Carlos Fuentes

The Lonely Hearts Club

Raul Nuñez

Bruñel meets Buster Keaton on the Ramblas.

A night porter in a sleazy Barcelona hotel, the only thing forty-year-old Antonio has going for him is his resemblance to Frank Sinatra. Thinking he has nothing to lose, he joins a lonely hearts club and into his life come a lonely widow, a dwarf poet and a gay barman.

The Lonely Hearts Club is a novel of Barcelona. Its people and its places, the Ramblas, the Plaza Real, the Barrio Chino, are brought to life in a book that is outrageously funny but never loses sympathy with its characters. First published fifteen years ago, it has become a cult classic.

'Its funny, dirty, sporadically grotesque and it's set in Barcelona. What more do you want?' *The Face*

'This tough funny story of low life in Barcelona manages to convey the immense charm of the city without once mentioning Gaudí. It veers between the sordid and the sentimental but, with a drunk's luck, never skids into either hole' *Independent*

'With its punchy language and outrageous surprises, Nuñez's work will appeal to all fans of the manic campery of Almodóvar's films' Patrick Gale

Adios Muchachos

Daniel Chavarría

Translated by Carlos Lopez

'Pulp fiction in Castro's Cuba. A picaresque novel with sex, scheming, and, well, more sex' Martin Cruz Smith

'Out of the mystery wrapped in an enigma that, over the last forty years, has been Cuba for the U.S., comes a Uruguayan voice so cheerful, a face so laughing, and a mind so deviously optimistic . . . Welcome, Daniel Chavarría' Donald Westlake

'If for no other reason than Daniel Chavarría and his novels of money, sex, and crime in Havana, the U.S. embargo against Cuba must end forthwith' Thomas Adcock

The beautiful Alicia hatches a plot to ensnare the wealthy foreign visitors to Castro's Cuba with an elaborate scam involving a broken bicycle and her voluptuous charms. Taking choreographed spills in front of expensive foreign cars, Alicia squeezes the maximum sympathy and cash out of her clueless, yet sexually aroused, victims. Add to this mix the guile of her mother, who is in on the scam, and the sky's the limit for Alicia. However, when she attempts to trap Victor, a convicted bank robber masquerading as a Canadian businessman, they quickly realise each other's nefarious motives and embark on a misadventure of sex, cross-dressing, kidnapping and death by olive.

Adios Muchachos is a dark, erotic, brutally funny romp through the underworld of post-revolutionary Cuba. It is the first English translation of a brilliant new voice in Latin American fiction.

Winner of 2002 Edgar Allan Poe Award for Best Paperback Original